Magnificent Mistakes

by Eric Bosse

Ravenna Press

2011

Support small presses and independent bookstores.

Published by Ravenna Press
Spokane, Washington USA
www.RavennaPress.com

FIRST EDITION

ISBN: 978-0-9835-9829-9
LCCN: 2011936160

Cover and book design by George Migash

Acknowledgments

Most of these stories are previously published, in earlier versions, some with alternate titles. I gratefully acknowledge the editors of *Absinthe Literary Review, Eclectica, Exquisite Corpse, Linnaean Street, Metazen, Mississippi Review, Night Train, Quick Fiction, Salt Flats Annual, Small Spiral Notebook, Snow Monkey, The Sun Magazine, Vestal Review, Wigleaf,* and *Zoetrope: All-Story Extra.*

And thank you to my mentors and teachers — Alexander Blackburn, Brady Udall, Dierdre McNamer, Debra Magpie Earling, Kevin Canty — to any number of generous readers — especially Pete Jones, Jim Ruland, Walker Hunter, Natalie Vaught, Elizabeth Hahn, Rose Gowen, Andrew Tibbetts, Jessie St. Amand, George Migash, and the house of tiny dreams — and to Kathryn Rantala. I must not forget to thank the University of Montana and the Merriam Frontier Foundation for their support. And I thank my wife, Rachel Losey, without whom I could not have made this book.

For Rachel

Contents

The Dog-Faced Boy

Two decades before he revolutionized the villanelle and transfigured the face of poetry, Gustave Bertaigne gained a reputation as the ugliest child in Philadelphia. His bulging eyes and grotesque proboscis only got uglier when his beard grew in so thick the neighborhood children nicknamed him "Rugface" and, later, "Wolfman," "Fuzzleface," and "The Hairy-Scary-Bloody-Mary-Huckleberry-Hound-Headed Boy." The pubescent poet complained to his diary that his whiskers felt "prickly and taut, like the quills of an angry, dead porcupine." When he shaved, the young Bertaigne's beard left notches in his father's straight razor. These notches sparked clashes between the boy and the man he knew as "Père."

One gray day, according to the diary, Père Bertaigne opened the door of their one-room cottage and caught his son belting a Vaudeville tune while hacking the razor through his whiskers. In a corner of the greasy mirror, Gustave glimpsed a fist flying at his head. The half-shaven boy ducked, but too late. The blow struck his ear with a thud and knocked him into the fetid bathing barrel. As he fell, an elbow clipped his wrist, and the straight razor sliced through the air and clattered into the piss bucket.

"God damn it, Bert!" Père's breath reeked of whiskey and the local butcher's ersatz sausage—half-cooked scraps of pork fat, garlic, and sage. "How much times do I must tell you not to use my razor?"

"But I need to shave, Père."

"Then buy your own self a razor, you stinking kid."

"No, Père, I do not stink." Gustave pointed a trembling finger at his father's shirt. "You stink."

Père's chest swelled to the size of the Liberty Bell. "Shut up, you peltface boy with the ugly of a dog from Hell! You get out of my house and never let me see your stinking, hairy face again!"

"I will!" Gustave pulled himself upright in the barrel. "I will go far to seek my fortune. But be warned, Père. Someday I will return to dump a sack of fine razors in your bed, throw you down on them, and use them to slice you to tidbits!"

His father reached into the mahogany-dark piss-water, grabbed the straight razor, and inspected its edge. "Again you nick my blade," he hissed. "I want nothing to do with you, you filthy mongrel." He lifted the boy from the barrel, booted his rump, and shoved him out the door, off the porch, and into the filthy street.

Gustave Bertaigne crawled to the gutter and dusted himself with hands still sticky with shaving soap. He glanced back at the ramshackle cottage as the front door slammed, sending up a wisp of dust.

As the dust sifted through the air—and, again, this comes to us via the young poet's private journal—a resplendent angel floated down from the clouds and swooped to the spot where Bertaigne cowered in the dirt. The angel had pale, emerald skin and yellow hair in curls about his shoulders. Or her shoulders—it was impossible to tell. The angel smelled of sweat and barbecue sauce. Its white wings somehow filtered and amplified the light of the sun. Bertaigne shielded his eyes and waited to be gathered up. He feared the angel had come to drag him to Hell for the words he had just spoken to his father. But nothing happened. Bertaigne looked again at the angel, who stood with its arms crossed, tapping its fingers on its biceps.

And the angel spake unto the young poet:

"Here, kid, take this."

The divine messenger's thunderous voice echoed in every language yet blew as softly as a breeze through reeds. The angel extended a hand. Between two fingers with chipped silver-painted nails, it held a small card with the words "FREAK SHOW" embossed in gold capital letters.

Bertaigne took the card. The angel ascended. As it did, it grew smaller and smaller until it became a glittering speck amongst the clouds. When that speck vanished, Bertaigne read aloud the paper card: "FREAK SHOW."

It was then that Bertaigne knew—as clearly as he knew, say, his own name or the proper sequence of lines in a villanelle—precisely how he would earn his living. His professional career would have little to do with poetry.

Years later, not long after a traveling menagerie of human oddities departed from Philadelphia, a neighbor found Bertaigne's elderly father dead in his bed. The old man had been slashed and dissected, and his body lay atop a pile of gleaming straight razors in a pool of crusty blood. The constable's only clue was a tattered sheet of paper pegged to the wall with a razor. The page bore nineteen hand-printed lines in six stanzas, with the first and third lines of the opening tercet recurring alternately at the ends of the subsequent tercets, and both lines repeated at the close of the final quatrain. Though the constable found the work mostly mediocre, he felt it revealed flashes of brilliance.

The Invisible World

Carolyn Farrier came to me with a strange look on her face. In fact, when she told me my mom was asking for me, all I could see of Carolyn was a pair of big brown eyes.

This was the summer between my fifth and sixth years of college. I had landed a job at the Atomic Bookshop. At around noon on my third day, the owner, Gene, asked me to "realphabetize" the cookbooks and shelve some new arrivals. "You'll find Cookbooks at waist level," he said, "under Gardening." So I wheeled my cart past Poetry and through Philosophy. Gene was right. Customers had left the cookbooks in disarray. I hummed the alphabet song, ignored a creepy feeling that someone was watching me, and slotted Jacques Pepin between the O's and Q's.

Then I saw Carolyn Farrier's eyes blink in the gap between the books and the shelf above. Carolyn was the shop's other employee. She had dirty blond hair, cut in the disheveled-hipster look of the day, and wore rectangular, black-framed glasses. She claimed to be eleven years older than I, but didn't look it. Because she had worked at the shop for three months, Gene appointed her to be my trainer. Her orientation course covered three topics: the art of not annoying Gene, the art of strategically annoying Gene, and the art of fooling Gene by looking busy while doing little.

When I spotted her eyes between the shelves, she whispered, "Someone wants you."

"And who might that be?" I asked, assuming this was flirtation and Carolyn was speaking of herself.

"Your mom," she said. "She's here with some dreadfully old man in tow."

I leaned toward the gap and asked Carolyn to tell my mom I had gone to lunch.

"No way," Carolyn said. "Gene told me to get you. Better hurry or your mommy might give you an early bedtime." She grinned as she said this.

I walked around the corner, and she reached out from Self Help to touch my arm.

"I was watching you," she said.

"I noticed."

At the checkout desk, Gene pecked at his calculator. My mom—decked in a lemon-yellow golf suit and sun visor—gripped my Grandpa Jerry by the sleeve of his pastel-blue coveralls. Grandpa Jerry wasn't Mom's father, but my other mother's travels often left Mom stuck with the old man.

"I know this is awful," she said, "I know, I know, but I have to do it."

I straightened the Dr. Strangelove postcard rack and tried to conjure up a bulletproof objection. Before I could speak, Carolyn jumped in.

"I found him in Cookbooks," she said from behind me.

Mom squinted at Carolyn then at me. "Your mother missed her flight again," Mom said. "She'll be home late."

Grandpa Jerry shrugged free of Mom's grip and reached for a volume of black-and-white nude photos on a shelf beneath the register.

I asked Mom what exactly she wanted from me. She shut the book in Grandpa Jerry's hands, put it back on the shelf, and tugged his wrist toward me.

"I can't stand this for another minute," she said. "Please just take him."

"Hey," Grandpa Jerry said. "I'm not a sack of potatoes."

Mom backed toward the door. "See you in three hours," she said.

I told her I'd love to help if I weren't on the job.

"Sorry," she said, "I'm sorry." And the door swung shut.

Carolyn chuckled. Gene scowled over the top of his glasses. Grandpa Jerry looked down at my hand on his wrist and followed the curve of my arm up to my shoulder. When he saw my face, he made a pop with his lips and asked if I knew of a White Castle in the neighborhood.

Gene covered the register, and Carolyn and I took Grandpa Jerry to the Velvet Freeze around the corner. As we walked, an ambulance cruised past at about ten miles per hour. The EMTs stared at us. "They should do a job," Grandpa Jerry said. When Carolyn asked

what he thought their jobs were, he said, "Picking up the pieces." A morbid laugh bubbled from Carolyn's throat. "What pieces?" Grandpa Jerry winked at me. "Pieces of the fools whose asses I've kicked."

Carolyn draped an arm over his shoulder. "Oh, I bet you kicked a lot of ass in your day," she said, "when you weren't dazzling the ladies."

"Ah, the ladies," Grandpa Jerry said. "I bet I've bedded more of them than this kid here"—he patted my hand—"has taken shits."

At the Velvet Freeze, Carolyn asked about my Mom and my mother.

"My mother is my biological mother," I said. "And my Mom is my mom."

"I'm confused," Carolyn said.

"Join the club," Grandpa Jerry said. He pulled a snapshot from his wallet and handed it to Carolyn. "This is Rose," he said. "My wife."

Carolyn brought the picture closer to her face then passed it to me. It was a faded, black-and-white, glamour shot of my late Grandma Rose. She reclined on a sofa, dressed in a sheer negligee, black panties, a garter belt, and black silk stockings. Her nipples were big and dark. She looked about thirty years old. I stuffed the wrinkled photo into Grandpa Jerry's wallet and paid with a check.

....

Later, a week into my book-shelving career, someone sneaked up behind me in Poetry. As I leafed through an old Norton Anthology of English Literature, Carolyn's half-whispered voice reached my ear before I knew she was there, inches behind me. She recited "To His Coy Mistress" from memory. But "recited" may not be the best verb to describe what she did. Carolyn planted that poem on my ears with her lips and her breath. She smelled faintly of fennel. I shut my eyes, and when she got to the bit about amorous birds of prey, her lips swooped down and grazed my neck.

After the poem, I pulled Carolyn's face to mine and kissed her. She turned away and said she was too old for a kid like me. I tried to kiss her again, but she walked past the customer bathroom and vanished into Fiction.

That evening, when our shift ended, Carolyn agreed to let me buy her dinner at La Creperie. The hostess seated us by the kitchen door. Carolyn ordered a bottle of Cotes du Ventoux, which arrived quickly, followed by Crawfish Etouffee to go with our strained conversation about favorite books, music, and films.

Then I asked about her wedding ring.

She scratched at a tiny wine stain in the tablecloth.

"Oh come on," I said. "Where's your husband?"

"The last of the international playboys?" she said. "He's on an extended business trip to Saudi, by way of Istanbul, via Rome, via London."

"What does he do?" I asked.

"He says he makes it rain, but really he watches changing oil prices and occasionally meets rich people for drinks. But let's not talk about him tonight."

"What's his name?"

"Simon."

"What's he like?"

Deltas of wrinkles tightened at the corners of her eyes. "He is deeply fucked up," she said. Under the table, her fingers found my knee. "What Simon doesn't see won't hurt him." Her chin tipped up and exposed her neck. She squeezed my thigh.

I flattened her hand on my leg and said it was a damn good thing Simon wasn't around. Carolyn raised her glass to that, and while I paid she stepped out to the sidewalk to make a call on her cell phone. I watched through the plate glass window as she chopped the air with her hands. When the call ended, she waved for me to follow.

And I did. I followed to where we had parked our cars. I followed her car through downtown into a cozy neighborhood north of the college. I followed up the walk to her front door. And I followed along a carpeted hallway to her bedroom, where we did things I was pretty sure Carolyn's husband would have killed me for, had he caught us.

She tore off my shirt, examined my chest, slid off my pants, told me to stand still, and stared at my legs. "Turn around," she said. "Very nice." She took off her glasses, folded them, and set them on the dresser. "Now, come here."

We kissed and rolled on the carpet awhile. My feet bumped her laundry basket. My fingers tangled in her hair. She stood and let her dress fall to her feet. I watched her exquisite body—full breasts, wide hips, a tiny paunch of a belly—move through the candlelight to a full-length mirror on a closet. And we both watched her caress her legs, her arms, and her neck.

She opened a dresser drawer and pulled out a wooden-handled brush with felt instead of bristles. She placed the brush on the floor in front of me, then got on her hands and knees and arched her back.

"Brush me," she said.

"Pardon?"

"I'm a pony. Brush me down."

"Wait," I said. I pointed at a picture frame on the nightstand. "Does he have to be here?"

The photo showed a big-nosed man in his thirties with a line of fuzz on his upper lip, smiling after blowing out a candle on a cupcake. He was seated at a table in a Mexican restaurant. He held a red napkin in one hand and a knife in the other. His teeth looked slightly too small for his mouth. Carolyn trotted over and put the picture in a drawer. Then she turned, leaned on the bed, and smiled. I flashed for a second on my Grandma Rose, posed for posterity in the warmth of Grandpa Jerry's wallet. But here was Carolyn, handing me a felt brush, guiding me to stroke her skin in small circles from her neck to her hindquarters. It took only a moment to banish Grandma Rose from my thoughts.

Now and then, during our equestrian training sessions, I wondered what Carolyn's husband would think if he saw me guiding his wife in tight circles around the arena of his bedroom. Gradually, though, I came to pretend Carolyn had no husband at all. She was my pony, I told myself, all else be damned. One night I guided Carolyn onto the bed and dropped her reins, eased the bit gag from her mouth, and slid the leather side straps down around her ears. Her head shuddered. She nuzzled her nose to my chest. When I had removed her gear and brushed her down, I rolled over and blew out the bedside candle. Smoke floated through the open window. My feet dangled over the edge of the bed, and I told Carolyn she should come to my place the next night.

She reached into the drawer for a pack of matches and lit the candle again.

"How's your grandpa?" she asked.

I told her he was fine, and again I said she should come over.

"I can't talk about it now," she said. "It's getting late. Time for you to go."

"Why?"

"Simon might call."

"In the middle of the night?"

"The time difference," she said. "It's confusing. But I should be here. And you should go." She kissed my hand.

I rested my head on her belly. Her intestines made dark, slippery sounds. She brushed her feathered plume across my cheek. "Come on," she said. "I'm sleepy."

"Do I have to go?"

"Does he have to go?" she asked the empty house.

....

That summer, I had rented a small room with a hot plate, a dorm fridge, and two closets, the larger of which housed a toilet and shower. Not long after the Fourth of July, I persuaded Carolyn to spend our lunch break at my apartment. We ate an entire bag of chips and onion dip. She paced the room and opened and shut the curtains. I asked what was wrong.

"Nothing," she said.

She put a hand on my cheek. Her fingers were moist. I patted the bed, smoothed the wrinkles in the sheet. She kissed me, and we made love then without hesitation, without straps, halters, mirrors, or candles—and without a picture of her husband tucked away in a nearby drawer. Then we did it again. And it was nothing like our equestrian events in her bedroom: no brush, no tack, no lingering by the mirror to shake her mane and admire her gear.

....

Back at the bookshop, Mom called to beg me to take Grandpa Jerry out so she could have a few hours to breathe. When I got to my parents' house, Mom stuffed eighty dollars in my hand and told me to keep him out as long as I possibly could.

Four hours later, at Murphy's Tavern, Grandpa Jerry ordered his fifth bourbon and slapped my shoulder. "What's your game, friend?" he said, trying to figure out who I was and how he knew me.

"Books," I said. "I work in books."

Grandpa Jerry nodded. "Publishing or writing?"

"Distribution."

"I'll be damned," he said. "It just so happens I'm a writer. Poems, mostly."

"Poetry, eh?" I sipped my beer. "What are your poems about?"

"Nature," he said. "And man-made things. I'm the best damn poet the world never heard of!" He laughed, slapped my shoulder again. The fat bartender gave me a look to say I'd better keep the old man under control.

Grandpa Jerry tapped the bar with his index finger. "To good times," he said. He picked up his glass and waved it around as if the room were full of dancing girls and happy drunks. But the only other customer was a tired trucker with a tattooed neck."

"Another bourbon!" Grandpa Jerry said, and he turned to me. "So, friend, what's your game?"

······································

It was late, past eleven, when I helped Grandpa Jerry out of my car and guided him up the driveway to my parents' house. A taxi pulled up along the street. My mother got out, paid the driver, walked over to us. "Well, well, well," she said. "Have you two been out on the town?"

"Alexandra!" Grandpa Jerry said. "I want you to meet my new friend." He whispered to me: "What's your name again, soldier?"

"We've met," my mother said. "How's it going, Ricky?"

"Well, meet him again!" Grandpa Jerry turned and introduced me to my mother. "This is my daughter, Alex. She's a doctor of some sort, and she thinks she's a man."

I shook my mother's hand, which was as big and strong as mine, but she didn't squeeze. In fact, she didn't do much besides flash her triumphant smile and tell us how great it was to see her father and son together in her front yard, no matter the hour. She laughed about how she'd get an earful from Mom for coming home so late. And she walked into the house, arm in arm with Grandpa Jerry, as if she and he had been the drinking buddies.

······································

Summer cantered along until August, when I found Carolyn at the bookshop, sitting on the floor in Eastern Religions, chewing on her lower lip. She had on jeans and a white sweater, and her hair was limp. I asked what was bothering her, and she tried to brush me off. When I pressed, she gave me a kiss and a hug.

I asked if she and Simon were splitting up.

"Oh no," she said, "nothing like that. We had a long talk, and we decided to start a family." She shook her head then shut her eyes. "There's something I haven't told you about him. Simon is not—he'd kill me for telling you this, but he's not someone who is physically able to have kids."

Several seconds passed before I thought to say, "Oh."

"I'm sorry," she said. "This has me all mixed up. I'm happy, though. Really happy."

"It's fine," I said. "I mean, it's none of my business, you know?"

"But it is," she said.

"How?"

She had taken off her glasses and was cleaning them by breathing on the lenses and wiping them with the T-shirt under her sweater. "Don't you worry about the baby," she said. "I'll take care of it."

"All right," I said. "Let's try not to panic."

....

Once, I came home from a high school party half drunk and fairly sure I had just lost my virginity. I slipped through the front door, stepped out of my shoes, and headed for the stairs. My mother's desk lamp gave off the only light in our dark house, so I tiptoed past her open study door. She cleared her throat, told me to come in and have a seat. "Do with this what you will," she told me, "but it is an irrefutable law of the universe." She shifted in her seat. Her hand rested, palm down, in the pool of light on the desktop. Her other hand swished a snifter of Scotch and ice. Her eyes were hidden by shadows. "That which we cannot see rules us," she said. She stared into her drink. "I mean particles, electrons, electromagnetic forces. Secrets. Love. Time. Fear. DNA. What we cannot see controls our lives." She picked up a pen, pointed it at me. "I know I haven't given you as much in this life as your Mom, but consider this my gift. And consider it fair warning: No one, nobody, no human being knows what rules us, Rick. We're all flying blind. Now go to bed." I reminded her that she had to sleep too. "Oh, I will," she said. "Just shut the door behind you."

....

In the predawn dark of my apartment, the force that ruled me was a shrieking telephone. I couldn't see it, but I could sure as hell hear it. I groped around, knocked Carolyn's water glass to the floor, and finally found the phone under the corner of the bed: "Hello?"

"Get the hell over here," Grandpa Jerry said. "Storm's coming and we've got rats."

"OK," I said. "It's the middle of the night."

"Night my ass. Sun's going down and we've got rats."

He hung up. I rolled over and kissed Carolyn's cheek. This was the first and only night Carolyn ever slept at my place. I had invited her dozens of times, and she had always passed. But when I pressed hard and threatened to confront Simon about our affair, she agreed to come over. As I kissed her, my stubble scraped her chin. She didn't flinch, though. All evening, I had tried to convince her to divorce Simon and move somewhere with me: California, Boston, Costa Rica, anywhere. She refused, though, and told me I'd probably actually get along with Simon if I ever met him. She had fallen asleep during my monologue about my vision for our future together.

I kissed her again, dressed quickly, ate a slice of cold pizza, and wrote a note: "Carolyn, Grandpa Jerry called. I need to make sure he and Mom don't kill each other. Back soon. You spent one night with me. On to the next and the next and the rest!"

....

I found Mom puffing a cigarette in her chair by the living room window. Yellow light seeped through the curtains, making her face look older than usual. Gray hair hung over her shoulders, and a crossword puzzle book sat open in her lap. She asked what I was doing there at that hour. I told her I'd written it on a cocktail napkin the other night and had given it to Grandpa Jerry. She glanced at her crossword and asked for a seven-letter word for betrayal, starting with P-E-R. I asked her what was in the cardboard box on the floor by the closet. She said it was filled with Grandpa Jerry's poems.

"Yesterday he packed to move to Chicago," she said. "Now he's in the back yard, building a wall with my flagstones." She waved a hand toward the rear of the house. "He's supposedly protecting us from rats. I'm telling you, he needs a nursing home."

....

Out on the deck, the breeze smelled of freshly turned dirt. Grandpa Jerry stood at the far end of the yard, beside a wheelbarrow. His crooked body bent over a row of pink flagstones. He had propped the bigger stones against smaller ones, making a short wall that faced a stand of junipers and scrub oaks between the yard and the bluffs. I cleared my throat. "Alexandra?" he said. His shoulders pulled inward, as if the act of looking up strained his neck. His tan coveralls were caked in dirt. He asked if I was his daughter, then told me we had rats out the wazoo but he was building a wall to keep the bastards out.

I invited him to come inside, but he pointed to the sky in the west. "You see those clouds?" he said. "That's the blackest herd of clouds I've ever seen. Know what that means?"

"Rain?"

"Hell yes. And when it rains, the goddamn rats will come for the house. You hear me?" He looked into my eyes and squeezed my right hand. His head trembled, and he waved me toward the wheelbarrow.

I stepped between the handles and lifted.

"Over there," he said, waving me toward the far end of the wall. I pushed, and he came along with the shovel. At a small stack of stones that had once formed the borders of Mom's flower garden, Grandpa Jerry dropped to his knees. His fingers hovered over a flagstone still flat in the ground, the last intact piece of the garden path. He wedged the shovel's scoop under the stone and leaned on the handle. The flagstone rose two inches then dropped. He scratched his arm. "Where is she?"

"Who?"

"My wife, dammit."

"Grandma Rose? She passed away fourteen years ago."

"I'm supposed to bring her strawberries." He rubbed his scalp with his palms then put a hand on my shoulder. "Who are you?"

....

I went back to my apartment. Carolyn was gone. A grocery receipt was taped to the fridge with a note written in pencil: "Richard, face facts. I'm married. You're in college. There's no future for us. Our time has come and gone. Please just forget you ever met me. I will quit the bookshop. Don't come to my house. And please don't bother my husband. He's a good man, and I love him. I'm sorry. Goodbye."

I sat with that note for a few minutes, then grabbed the last slice of cold pizza and ate as I drove. "Face facts?" I said to the empty car. "What facts?"

....

Carolyn's front door stood open a few inches. I knocked and, after a while, stepped inside. The house was quiet, so I went down the hall. A toilet flushed as I passed the closed door of the bathroom, so I went into the bedroom to wait for Carolyn. But she was there, sitting with her back to the mirror on the closet door.

When she saw me, she jumped up and started pushing me out of the room.

"Leave," she said.

"Who's in the bathroom?" I asked.

"You need to leave."

"He's here," I said, and stood my ground.

Down the hall, the bathroom door opened. I heard squeaks and bumps. Carolyn stopped pushing and sat on the bed with her hands on her knees.

When I turned, I saw Simon in the doorway. For a second I thought he must be terribly short, but he sat in a wheelchair. His legs were thin and bent. His nose looked smaller in person than in the photo, which was now in its proper place on the nightstand.

"What is he doing here?" Simon said.

I started to introduce myself.

"I know who you are," he said.

"What are you doing home?" I asked.

He shook his head. "I never left." He smiled at Carolyn, who walked over and stood beside his chair. When she placed her hand on his shoulder, I felt suddenly and inexplicably tender toward him.

"Please leave," Carolyn told me.

I sat down on the bed. Simon's face went bright red then faded to pale. Carolyn started to speak, but he cut her off. "I'll do the talking," he said. He nodded at me. "I don't know how you talked my wife into staying at your place last night, but that's not going to happen again."

"Believe me," I said, "things between me and Carolyn are not over."

"They're about to be." He pointed at the closet door. "Open it. Go on."

I thought I ought to leave before this escalated into some kind of wrestling match on wheels, but he didn't seem angry. So I went to the closet door and opened it.

At first I saw only lines, angles, and tiny reflections of metal and plastic and convex glass. As the door swung open, the closet's contents came into the light: various cameras stood on tripods—a camcorder, a 35 mm Nikon, what appeared to be an 8 mm movie camera like the one my mother used to fiddle with on road trips. A white plastic lawn chair sat behind the tripods, and beside the chair was a small table with a glass of water, a jar of Vaseline, and a sketch pad. Carolyn's clothes hung to the left of the cameras. Simon's shirts, pants, and ties hung on the other side. The closet was nearly as big as my apartment.

"You were here every night," I said.

Simon apologized for any pain the situation might have caused. This was a private thing, he told me, between him and his wife—nothing personal against me. He assured me the pictures would never leave his hands. "But Carolyn and I didn't anticipate what happened," he said. "We should have, but we didn't."

"And what happened?" I asked.

"She fell in love with you," he said. "I'm so sorry."

Carolyn did not make eye contact with me. She came around and pushed Simon's wheelchair toward the bed. He reached down and flipped a brake, and the wheels locked. Carolyn pushed harder, but the chair wouldn't budge.

"What are you doing?" he said.

She didn't say anything. She just stood there, staring at the back of his head.

I walked past them and reached under the bed for Carolyn's plastic tote full of reigns, blinders, bits, and gags. I set the tote on the bed and removed the lid.

"So you knew about all of this?" I said. "All along?"

Simon nodded. "It was kind of my idea," he said.

Carolyn sat down and sobbed. I felt the summer slipping through my fingers, felt her falling into an abyss.

....

I drove to a park and sat on a bench for a couple hours. I watched children whirling around orange and white playground equipment, hurtling through the air on swings and slides. I lay back and tried to sleep. Sunlight glowed wild red through my eyelids. I took in the shouts, voices, and bird songs. A car door clicked open and shut. A squirrel chattered. A block or two down the road, someone slammed a dumpster lid. Farther away, a train whistle blew. As the sun drifted, leaf shadows flickered over my tired eyes. I wondered why I didn't feel more angry or ashamed, why the greater portion of my sadness came not from what I had done but from what I had failed to see. The little kids and their mothers cleared out for lunch, and the office workers started showing up: men in ties, with their jackets off; women in navy-blue dresses, carrying brown paper sacks.

I felt hungry, and I got into the car with every intention of going to my apartment. But I drove back to Carolyn and Simon's house. I parked on the street and tried to work out whether to burn their house down or knock on the door and ask if there was anything I could do to help get ready for the baby.

From the Canyon to the Driveway

The woman tossed her shirt onto a rock in the sun. Water curved over and around her body as she stepped into the falls, and Ethan felt in his gut how savage he could be if he had the nerve to step out from behind the scrub oak. The woman hummed as she showered, and Ethan counted the sounds he could hear: (one) her voice, (two) the whistle of water as it churned the rocks and settled into the stream bed, (three) the shrieks of crows chasing a hawk from a bluff, (four) the drone of a jet plane, (five) the buzz of a prop plane, (six) wind in the aspen leaves, (seven) his fingers crinkling the wrapper on the baseball-card pack in his pocket, (eight) the chatter of insects, and (nine) heavy footsteps approaching from behind.

Ethan knew the stuttered rhythm of his father's walk. After one last glance at the woman, who was watching him now and covering herself with her hands, Ethan scrambled up the rocks. He cut back onto the trail just as the old man slogged around a switchback.

"Hey, bud, there you are," his father said. He stopped and unbuttoned his shirt. "Didn't think I'd see you till I got back to the car."

"Yup," Ethan said. "I'm here."

His father wiped his neck with a bandana, blew his nose, and stuffed the rag into his pocket. "So, Mr. E., you got an answer for me?"

Ethan whizzed a flat stone at a pine tree. The stone glanced off a branch and knocked a hail of brown needles into the weeds.

"Damn," his father said. "Looks like you inherited the old man's arm. Hey, look, Ethan, take your time. It's a big decision. Answer me when you're ready."

They walked downhill, and Ethan went first.

"All-time all-stars," his father said. "Behind the plate: Johnny Bench or Yogi Berra?"

"Pudge."

His father gave him a playful shove in the back. "Don't yank my chain, punk."

"Seriously," Ethan said over his shoulder. "Bench is like eighty years old. And Yogi Berra's dead, right?"

"Yeah yeah, ha ha, very funny."

"Pudge hit .340 with twenty homers last year."

"No way in hell did that slouch hit .340."

"Swear to god."

"OK, was your Mister Pudge ever voted MVP? I think not."

"In the NLCS he was."

"Oh big whoop."

They went on like this for half an hour, with Ethan drafting from a pool of players whose faces would have meant nothing to him on the street or in a police line-up. His father cracked wise about steroids, Coors Field, and corked bats. At the trailhead, the old man cracked open a beer and spun the car backward, away from a green Saab that probably belonged to the woman at the waterfall.

"I know I told you to take your time," Ethan's father said, "but I do want an answer when we get to the house."

Ethan settled into the cracked vinyl of the passenger seat and stared up at the strip of blue sky between the treetops. "What's the difference between a crow and a raven?" he asked.

His father tossed his cigarette butt out the window. "Hell," he said, "ravens are bigger, and they've got kind of a mane of feathers around their necks."

The car slipped from the woods of the canyon into a jumble of streets and houses. Ethan's father punched in the cigarette lighter. A few seconds later, it popped out, fell on the floor, rolled over pebbles and note cards, and came to rest against Ethan's shoe.

"Watch your foot," his father said.

"Bench," Ethan said. "I'd go with Bench."

This drew a chuckle and a pat on the shoulder. His father reached for the lighter and popped it into place. At a stoplight, two high-school girls in halter tops and mini-skirts crossed in front of the car. Ethan's father shut his eyes.

"What I wouldn't give to be seventeen again," he said.

"What were you like?" Ethan asked.

"What do they say—young, dumb, and full of cum? Whatever I was, I was not nearly the gentleman you're going to be at that age, I can tell you."

Ethan reached across the stick shift, nestled his hand into the hollow between his father's neck and shoulder, and counted sounds all the way home.

In the driveway, his father pulled the E-brake and let the engine idle. He shifted to face Ethan. "Well, bud, what's it going to be?"

Ethan looked at his shoes.

"Mom," he said. "But I will visit. A whole lot. Every weekend."

His father shuddered as the breath left his lungs. He released the brake and jammed the stick into reverse but held the clutch long enough for Ethan to climb out and shut the door. Long enough for Ethan to walk to the driver's side and peck his father on the cheek. Long enough for Ethan's mother to fry chicken and take his father a drumstick on a paper plate. Long enough for the sky to grow dark and for the engine to sputter and stop.

A Puff of Smoke

The moon bubbles and melts in the window of Scott's Volkswagen Beetle. He, Danny, Alana, and I are parked at Fort Missoula Cemetery in the rain, with the Violent Femmes blasting on the stereo and the seats buzzing our backs. Scott sports a bleached blond Mohawk. Danny's got three safety pins for earrings and jagged mascara to make his eyes pop. And Alana shakes her mango-colored hair to the beat. She sits beside me in the backseat, and her jeans rub mine. Danny leans back and holds a joint in my face. I wave it off with my good hand through cobwebs of smoke.

"Come on, Dinosaur," he says. "You know I care about you, right?"

"Fuck yeah I do," I say, but I know he doesn't give a damn about me.

"So try it," Danny says. "If it sucks, you never have to do it again."

Scott, who hasn't spoken in ten minutes, nods with this look like if the joint sucks then he too might never smoke again. His Mohawk brushes the dome light.

Alana's hair sticks to the window. She's high and absentmindedly strokes my leg with her fingers. This feels good but creepy because she's gawking at gravestones and has a thin track of spittle on her chin.

"Quit drooling, dope fiend," Danny says.

Alana wipes her mouth with a sleeve. She smiles at me. "You gonna smoke, sweetie?" She puts a hand on my chest and says, "You don't have to."

But she's wrong. I do. It's time. I take the joint in my fingers. It feels like a warm, dead moth. I suck on it. Nothing happens. Scott flicks his lighter and singes my nose hairs.

"Breathe in," Alana says. "Hold it."

I hold it till my lungs rage and I choke.

As I cough, Alana takes my stubby left hand and puts it in her lap. Danny and Scott face forward again and we all sit there watching rain slither down the windows.

"Hey, Dino," Danny says. He turns to talk to me. "I don't get it. Why'd your dad blow out his brains if he was such an awesome fucking guy and all?"

Alana smacks his head and says, "I'm hungry for Pop Tarts."

"Cinnamon," Scott says. He sits up, raises his seat, and starts the car. Five minutes later, we pull up to Rosauers Supermarket. The lights in the store are so bright they hurt. I don't want to go in. "I'm high," I say, but I'm not really high. Not yet. "I'll just crash by these fertilizer bags."

Alana gives me a hug and peers into my eyes. "You OK, Dino?"

"Just dandy," I say.

So they go inside, and I sit on a pallet of Weed & Feed. The Coke machine glows red on the wet sidewalk. The handicapped parking space's paint is chipped and faded. A bald guy with a white isosceles triangle mustache comes out of the store, smiles, and walks over to me. He has a carton of chocolate milk in one hand and a pack of Dolly Madison buns in the other.

"Hey there," he says. "How do you like this town?"

"It's all right," I say.

"How long you been here?"

"Three years," I say.

"Yeah? Where'd you come from?"

"Cleveland."

The guy winks. He's got a blue Oxford shirt like the one my dad used to wear, and it's peculiar to see basically Dad's shirt on some old bald guy.

Two jocks in a black Mustang cruise through the lot. I don't recognize them. The driver has a roll of fat like a hot dog bun around his neck. He tosses a cigarette at the pavement and cranks a Def Leppard tune. His arm hangs out the window and his fingers wiggle in the rain. The Mustang squeals out of the lot and heads south on Reserve, toward the golf course.

The bald guy chuckles. "What's your name?"

I think for a second. "Kurt."

"Hi, Kurt. I'm Roy." Roy looks at me like he's trying to remember where we met before. "Do you know Jesus?"

I take a deep breath and finally the pot hits me. My fingers go numb and my lips get all fat. "Not personally," I say. I can hardly spit out the words.

"I don't mean to pry, Kurt. I'm just in town, visiting my daughter." He waves his pack of buns at the neighborhood across the street. "I thought I'd stroll over for a midnight snack. Couldn't help but notice the questionable crowd you arrived with."

"Questionable?" I say.

"They seemed sort of wild, is all."

"Oh, they're a pack of wild animals, all right," I say. Or that's what I try to say. I'm not convinced that Roy can understand me, with my lips feeling all blubbery and wet.

He goes on for a while about the Gospel of John and the afterlife and how good deeds aren't enough because Heaven isn't something we earn, Heaven is a gift given by the grace of God. Roy knows I'm the reason the Lord brought him here tonight. He can feel it.

A stick of gum, still in its silver foil, lies on the sidewalk next to Roy's foot. I reach out, but Roy steps on the gum.

"You seem like a nice kid. Tell me, Kurt, were you born like that?"

"Yep," I say and hold up my stubby hand.

Roy's white mustache curls with his smile. "Well, maybe the Lord will bless you with two good hands in the afterlife. Would you like that?"

"I wouldn't know," I say, because I have spent my entire life trying and failing to imagine a different set of fingers.

"I bet you would," Roy says. "What church do you go to?"

I tell him the first one that comes to mind. It was a place we went one Easter, back in Cleveland: "First Methodist." It had a brick fireplace in the back, behind all the pews. During the service, a fat guy in a polyester suit tossed logs on the fire.

Roy sips his chocolate milk. "Do they talk about being born again at First Methodist?"

I scratch an itch on my ankle.

"Well, you're what? Fifteen? I was all of thirty-three before I figured out that warming a seat in church did not get me one step closer to Heaven. Then, Kurt, I decided to let my Lord and Savior into my heart, and never, not once, did I look back. Every single day is a gift, I tell you. Every day." Roy steps closer. "Do you have any idea what I am talking about?"

"Not really."

"Revelations says Jesus is coming to separate the good from the bad, Kurt. The goats will end up on one side of the fence, and the sheep will wind up on the other. If that happened tonight, Kurt, if Jesus came down to judge you right now, right this very minute, which side of the fence would you be on?"

"I don't believe in a magical fence," I say. "But I try to be a good person."

Roy balances his milk carton in his hand. "That's not biblical, Kurt. When Jesus comes, your goodness and your niceness won't have anything to do with anything. The true believers will vanish in a puff of smoke and the unbelievers will be cast down into eternal flame. Do you hear me?"

"I hear you," I say. I also hear the hiss of cars out on Reserve and the rumble of thunder up in the mountains.

"You can choose your side of the fence, Kurt, right here, right now. You know what day this is?" Roy raises his package of buns above his head. "Today is the day the Lord has made, Kurt. Today is the day you are going to change your life."

It's just me and Roy and some mentally disabled kid in a blue apron pushing a train of grocery carts toward the automatic doors. I'm standing up now, but I don't remember getting up. Roy has his arm around my shoulder. His eyes are dark green and too close to mine. His breath is coffee and puke and cinnamon and yeast.

"Kurt, buddy, let's drive a stake in the ground right now. From this day forward, you will walk with the Lord. It's so simple. There's no need to even close your eyes or anything. Will you take my hand right now and open your heart to Jesus with me, Kurt?"

Roy has splotches on his forehead. He looks gloomy but hopeful, like he's trying to change his luck even though he knows he can't. And I want to make him happy. So I imagine having long, full, regular fingers instead of stubby ones. This makes me laugh, and not because it's funny but because all of a sudden I feel fingers on the end of my left hand. I clench my imaginary fist. I wriggle the digits.

But Roy seems worried.

"You look peculiar," he says. "Are you sick? Are you all right, Kurt?"

I try to stop laughing. "Which ones are the goats?" I ask.

"Forget about the goats," he says.

"No. You said Jesus sorts out the sheep and the goats. Are the goats on the Heavenly side of the fence or the Hell side? Because I hate goats. I hate sheep more, so I guess I'd rather be a goat."

Then Danny and Scott start making goat sounds or maybe sheep sounds. They waggle their heads and bleat at the sky. Alana has one foot on a grocery cart and she's spinning in circles through the handicapped parking spot. I laugh and snot flies out of my nose and lands next to the stick of gum on the sidewalk. The gum still has Roy's boot print in it.

I look for Roy. He's walking away with the buns I had hoped he'd offer if I agreed to let Jesus into my heart. Roy cuts through the parking lot and stops at the crosswalk. Danny tells us to get in the car. Roy jogs across the median. He doesn't turn to wave goodbye. I climb into the car and put my head on Alana's lap. I slide my arm under her leg and reach for her ankle. And they are gone — my new fingers — as quick as they came.

The Aborted Documentary

A static-filled screen flashes to a head shot of a mother seated on a maroon-and-gold ottoman. Medium-plump with tightly permed curls and oversized bifocals, she wears a pink sweatshirt under a green and red checked apron. Her face features the prominent lower lip and cocked eyebrow of a matron coerced by her progeny into sitting before a video camera.

The filmmaker's voice, resolute and quasi-formal, addresses her from off-camera: "Ready?"

Her eyes widen with dread, and she shrugs her shoulders.

"Here's the deal, Mom. Talk about me as if I died last week. You've got two minutes. Go."

Her eyebrows rumple toward the bridge of her nose. She draws a quick breath, audible over the murmur of a television in another room.

"Go ahead," her son says. "I'm dead. Run with it."

She glances into the lens, then at her lap. "What do you mean?" she asks.

"I mean, I died last week, and now there's a documentary film crew interviewing you about me."

"Oh, you and that damn camcorder," she says.

"Talk *about* me, Mom, not *to* me. And could you set down that drink?"

"Jesus Christ," she mutters and puts her glass on the end table. "He was a very good boy." She folds her fingers together in her lap and gazes off toward the kitchen.

"That's it? That's all you've got?"

"What more do you want?" she asks.

"I don't know. Something a bit less boring?"

"Oh, you want interesting?" She picks up her drink, downs the last swallow of vermouth, and spins the ice in the glass. "I'll give you interesting."

"Please do."

"He *thought* he got away with things."

"Like what?"

"Oh, believe me," she says, "you don't want to know."

"Sure we do."

She raises her chin and glares at the camera. "No you don't."

"Mom, this project will only work if you tell the truth. So, what sorts of 'things' did he think he got away with?"

"This," she says and waves her cupped hand in the universal gesture for masturbation. "That boy kept nudie magazines under his mattress and played with himself three, four, five times a day, every day, up until the day he died."

"Mother—"

"He'd do it in his bedroom or the bathroom or even in the TV room when he thought no one knew he was watching those sexy movies."

"All right, all right. Stop. Enough." After a long pause, in which the mother's face spreads into a callous smirk, the filmmaker asks, "Did he do anything you'll remember him for?"

She considers this. "Not really."

"Oh, come on, Mom."

She shrugs again. "Well, he tried acting, music, even writing for the local paper, but he wasn't very good. Not really. Not in a way that anyone would take notice." She gives the camera a wink. "He was mainly just a kid who never appreciated his mother and shot his wad into bath towels, which she then had to haul from his bedroom and pile into the washing machine."

The camera tilts toward the floor where, for a split second, it captures a blurry view of the mother's worn, white sneakers and the frayed cuffs of her pant legs. The image shudders into a flurry of black-and-white snow.

The Master of Submission

Chess wakes to tingle in his nose. He reaches to scratch it, but his wrists chafe against their metal cuffs. Suspended horizontally in a sling three feet above the floor, he pulls down on the handcuffs to ease tension on the testicle belt. He then extracts his left foot from its stirrup. The foot dangles, and his weight shifts, which tightens his torso harness. To compensate, he thrusts his pelvis. But this cranks the testicle belt tighter—a major design flaw. "Goddamn frack," he says—but the ball gag makes his words come out as "Mmm-mmmm mmph!" Then last night comes rushing back. He asked Priti to strap him into the device moments before she walked out of his world forever. How had she put it?

"This phase of my life ends now."

"What phase?" he asked.

"The warped, psychotic phase."

Then she cinched a nylon rope to the bed frame and looped it through the torso harness. Though Chess had not designed the device with auxiliary ropes in mind, he went with it. Now, in more pain than he has ever known, he lifts his right foot from its stirrup and kicks at the release switch on the primary crossbar. He misses and flops sideways, but kicks again. This time his foot hits squarely on target. And the device's accessories click and release: first the wrist cuffs then the arm binder, the latex surrender collar, and the locking rubber knee separator. On cue, the suspension swing lowers him to the floor. He unsnaps the ball gag and spits it from his mouth then removes the testicle strap. He unties Priti's surprise nylon rope, retracts the secondary crossbar, folds the device downward and inward, and stuffs it into a suitcase in the closet.

"Dear god," Chess whispers, "what have we done?"

He grabs a towel, puts a bagel in the toaster, and goes for a shower.

When he gets back to the kitchen, he finds no cheese in the fridge. And no eggs. Priti must have tossed them. He picks up his phone and sends a text: "Did u veganize again?" His nose tingles. He sends another text: "I miss u." And another: "Sorry. I will stop. Goodbye." Standing before the mirror in skinny black jeans and a trench coat, he feels overcome with love and gratitude for Priti. So he texts, "Thank u for everything." Then, hands tucked in pockets, eyes angled low, he heads out the door. He trudges up and down every glistening corridor of the mall and lingers awhile at the food court, hoping Priti will stop by for a falafel. She does not. "I wish u a lifetime of bliss," he texts. Then he cruises the coffee shops, music shops, head shops, and porn shops on Colfax and walks over to the deserted Greyhound station, which reeks of piss and chlorine. "Ick!" he texts. "Bad smells!" Then he texts, "Sorry! Not u. LOL" Then, "Icky bus station." Then, "ROFL!" Then, "Am sad. Not ur problem. Love u. Bye."

He returns to the apartment five hours after he left. "Plz call me, Mistress," he texts. "I still have pics of u pegging me." He eats a burrito and smokes cigarettes as fast as he can roll them. His nostrils itch. When he rubs them, they hurt. Just before midnight, his phone emits three whip cracks. It's her.

"Hey," she says all chipper and warm. "Would you *please* delete the pegging pics and stop texting me?"

"My nose hurts," he says. "I'm in pain, Mistress."

"I'm not your mistress anymore. Don't call me that."

"Where are you?" he asks.

"Why did you make me cuff you into your stupid device last night?"

"So I wouldn't stalk you," he says.

"Oh," she says in that sarcastic schoolgirl voice that would be cute if it weren't so devastatingly sexy. "Just do your breath meditation."

"I don't need anger control."

"The other one," she says, "for migraines: *out with the poison, in with the love.*"

"I'm drowning here, Priti."

"Take aspirin. Goodbye."

"Wait." Chess presses his wrist to his forehead. "I don't know how to be alone."

"You're not. You have your device."

"I don't need the Master. I need you to tie me up and punish me. You're my top, Priti, and you will always be my top."

"I am not your top anymore and you'll always be a passive-aggressive control freak," she says. "Destroy those pics or I will kill you."

The line clicks.

"Deleting them now," he texts. "And I will always be ur bottom."

Then he crumples to the floor and does some migraine-relief breathing: *out with the noxious poison of life, in with the golden luminescence of love.* It doesn't work. His headache settles in. And his nose burns. And he's a worthless speck of crap who should delete the photos and stop ruining Priti's life. But the thing is, she is his mistress. They were so good together. And they could be good again. And his nose never hurt before she left. He must win her back. After midnight, he goes to the closet, pulls out the Master of Submission, unfolds the device, and fastens himself in to sleep.

....

At work, a framed snapshot sits on the receptionist's desk, showing her pudgy adult children seated at a picnic table with jaundiced babies in their laps. In the photo, they all have barbecue sauce on their shirts, and the whole mob seems to find this funny. Their mouths contort with laughter.

"All that sauce could be blood," Chess says, "It looks like they're clawing their children to shreds. Oh, did I just say that out loud?"

"Not funny," the receptionist says. "What's the matter with my poor little Chessie Poo, anyway? He looks so glum."

"Chessie Poo feels like someone drizzled carbolic acid into his nasal cavity," he says, and he loosens his necktie. "Plus, despite Chessie Poo's superpower to get anyone to do anything he wants, his girlfriend dumped him on Saturday night."

"Oh, sweetie, I'm sorry," she says. "For the nose, go see a doctor."

"I don't have insurance."

"You do."

"I've never used it."

"Don't you read your pay stub?"

"I signed up for e-deposit."

"Then you get an e-stub," she says. "You also receive a link to an updated directory of system physicians every six months. And I bet a nickel my poor little Chessie Poo carries a member ID card in his wallet."

He hands her the wallet. She fishes out the card, pulls up the URL for the directory of physicians, and emails it to him.

"Psych," he says. "And thanks. You just saved me ten minutes of research."

"Ooh," she says, "my little Chessie Poo pulled a fast one."

Twenty minutes later, on his way out of the office, Chess sends Priti a text: "Off 2 see doc re: nose pain." And another: "Come back or I post pegging pics online." And another: "Sent flowers to ur parents house. Red roses & black tulips. Ur fav."

....

Framed photos of Dr. Kaplan's family clutter the walls of the examining room: his emaciated wife and bucktoothed kids looking nauseous at the Rock of Gibraltar; he and his wife grinning in the mist of a massive waterfall; the whole family propping up the Leaning Tower of Pisa. They seem so peaceful and so not-in-intense-nose-pain. And here's Dr. K himself, in a white coat, pressing an otoscope into Chess's nose. A mentholated lozenge rattles in Dr. K's mouth. With moist fingers, he pokes Chess's ribs, prods his belly, and asks if any of this hurts. It does not.

"Just my nose," Chess says.

Dr. K clears his throat. "OK, may I offer something personal here? It's important that you hear this from a stranger who knows nothing about you except that you're allergic to penicillin."

"Go on," Chess says.

"I visit with many patients. When I travel the world, I see many people. I fancy myself a keen observer of human behavior." He takes another lozenge from his pocket and pops it into his mouth. "With that in mind, you are—or, rather, you appear to be—conspicuously, perhaps even intentionally, oh, let's say, morbid. Down in the dumps. Depressed. It's as if you *cultivate* the appearance of mortal despair. Plus, the eyeliner is just odd."

"Can I go now?" Chess says.

Dr. K. writes a prescription for 200 milligrams of Asinil. "Twice a day every day for five weeks," he says and hands the slip to Chess.

"Your co-pay's fifty dollars," the nurse says and takes his debit card.

"$38.95," the cashier behind the counter at the drugstore says. She's sluggish and droopy-eyed, with hair held in a bun by chopsticks. And she's young. And thin. And kind of edgy looking, in a sexy-librarian-in-a-lab-coat way. On a whim, as she passes him his receipt, Chess reaches over the counter to pull out the chopsticks. She flinches and retreats behind a shelf. Then she calls over the P.A. for the manager. Chess rushes out of the store, cursing his stupid lack of impulse control.

In the car, he washes down the Asinil with a chocolate cream soda and waits for the pain to stop. It doesn't. For several minutes, he sits there and feels no change in nose pain whatsoever and tries not to punch himself in the face. It's maddening. He prefers to pick and choose his pain. He wonders how many pills he would have to take to kill himself. He hits the dashboard. What hurts deeply is not so much his nose. It's this: What would happen if Priti walked past right now, by pure chance? Even if she saw him, even if they made direct eye contact and saw into each other's souls, Priti would see his pain and refuse to get into his car. Which would be pathetic enough. But, knowing her, she wouldn't be alone. She would have some new guy on her arm.

His phone buzzes. It's a text: "Post even 1 of those pics online and u will die."

"I am a bad boy, Mistress," he texts. "Spank me."

And he follows that with about a dozen texted apologies and promises to go straight home and delete the photos from his hard drive.

Back at his apartment, he backs up the photos on a flash drive and hides it in the bathroom medicine cabinet, behind a tube of anti-itch cream. For good measure, he burns the files onto five CDs which he tucks into drawers and under cushions around the apartment. Then he slices his black leather pants, patches the slice with a dozen safety pins, and heads over to Goth Night at Club Forsaken. At ten o'clock, the club lives up to its name. A couple of ghoulish fags make out at the bar; a dominatrix commands a middle-aged bald guy to lick her boots in the far corner; and DJ Lugosi sways to an Eternal Deformity remix in his black-lit booth above the dance floor. Chess orders an ice-water and sits at a table behind the go-go cages. From there he'll be able to spot Priti if she comes in, but she won't see him. As he waits, he rubs his nose with ice chips.

An hour later, Raven—friend and ex-lover of Priti's—descends the stairs in knee-high black boots, a red corset, and a black mini-skirt shredded at the hem above fishnet stockings. The club throbs with sweaty freaks, and Raven is ordering a drink at the bar when Chess gets to her. He grabs her elbow.

"Where's my Mistress?" he says.

"Hands off, little perv boy!" she says. A smug grin bends her blackened lips. She hunches over her phone and texts someone.

Chess covers her phone with his hand. "Where's Priti?"

Raven cocks her head like she's thinking hard. "Priti? Why?"

"She told me she's never coming back."

"Ah!" Raven chuckles. Her eyes go wide. "Then you need a new mistress. Visit my dungeon. Tonight. Bring your own collar and this device of yours I've heard so much about."

He considers this. In many ways, Raven offers an adequate replacement for what he has lost. But she is Raven. She is not Priti. "I don't know," he says. "Maybe it's too soon."

Raven gives his earlobe a bite. "Your heart knows nothing yet of the depth of your own pain," she whispers, and she seeps into the crowd.

....

The next morning, Chess buys a latte and a blueberry scone in the lobby at work and takes them to the roof. It's a gray day. He sits on the parapet and dangles his legs. The nostril pain is gone, but the nasal swelling has increased. The bushes and trees around the office campus look artificial from up on the roof. Even the marble fountain in the plaza looks like a digitized simulation of water. Chess could probably jump into it. Actually, he could just slide forward a few inches and goodbye cruel, quasi-holographic world. But the scone tastes good. And the latte is all right.

"This is it," he texts to Priti. "If u do not come back 2nite, I send pegging pics to friends." He looks at the sky. "I am a bad boy," he texts. "Punish me."

A chubby Greek or possibly Italian woman steps out of the stairwell. She has long, dark hair and awe-inspiring cleavage, and she's not chubby-fat, exactly, but sort of chubby-thin like an old movie starlet. She takes a deep breath of freshly polluted air, and she wrinkles her nose. She coughs, looks at Chess, and gives him a shy, well-here-we-are wave. He waves back. She sets her coffee on the parapet. He looks at the coffee, then down at the fountain, then back at her.

"Don't jump," she says.

"Crossed my mind."

"Well then," she says, and pulls a pack of cigarettes from her purse. "I guess it's up to me to talk you out of it." Her voice is a touch deep and breathy, and her navy-blue suit dangles open at the lapels. "What's your name?"

"Chess."

"Hi, Chess," she says. "This is going to sound weird—"

"I'm down with weird," he says.

"Good. Has anyone ever told you that you have an extremely sexy nose?"

Chess rolls his eyes and the he stained-glass sky ripples like someone skipped a rock across it.

"Hmm," he says and touches his nose. "Not to my face." He dips his scone in his latte and stares at the buildings glittering in the distance.

"I'm surprised," she says, "But, then again, I'm freakishly attracted to big noses."

Chess checks his watch. As he swings his legs back over the parapet, he spills his latte. The woman reaches for it but taps it in the other direction. The cup tumbles through the air and just misses a cart of vending machine snacks. The vending machine supply guy looks up and flips off the roof. The woman touches Chess's arm and hands him her card: ORNELLA DELVECHHIA, ACCOUNT REPRESENTATIVE

"Call me," she says.

"OK." Chess pockets her card. "I probably will."

"Good."

In the elevator, he's thinking that if Priti had any idea some Mediterranean chick with a nose fetish had given him her business card and said, "Call me"—hoo boy! Jealousy made Priti horny. In fact, it made her crazy. Like that night at Wet Willie's Wonder Palace when a voluptuous blonde in knee socks and a plaid skirt kept asking Chess if he wanted a lap dance, and all he said was "Maybe later" every time she came to the table, until Priti went all shock-and-awe on the poor stripper, spitting and hissing and shouting so loud the bouncer threw Priti over his shoulder and dumped her in the parking lot. That was the first night she tried anal beads on him (or, rather, in him), and the first night she snapped cuffs around his wrists.

In the men's room mirror, Chess examines his nose. It's pinkish in the bridge region, and the nostrils look perhaps more than slightly swollen. But intensely handsome? His stomach flutters. Could be the Asinil or the scone or the business card. Who the hell likes big noses, anyway?

Back at his desk, Chess texts Priti: "Pics deleted. Done with U. Found new girl."

Priti replies: "Good. Now fuck off."

....

Several fat families with fat kids are crammed, fat upon fat, on benches in the foyer of Davey's Downtown Bistro: An American Dining Experience, so Chess and Ornella wait at a mini-table in the bar until a regular dining-room table becomes available. This place was Ornella's idea, and he's determined to go with the flow. He wears no eyeliner, for instance. And no nail polish. The place reeks of onion rings and mozzarella sticks. Ornella sips a Chocolate Rum-A-Dum-Dum through a straw then orders another. Between sips, she lightly caresses Chess's nostrils.

"Wow," he says, trying to get into it. "I've never been touched like this."

"Lucky for me," she says. Her hands smell like bubble gum. He's thinking, Go, Ornella, go! And at the same time he's wondering what Priti would do if she saw him now. Would she rip Ornella's eyes out? Or would she slap his face and make him crawl to the car then whip his ass until he begged for mercy and order him to sleep naked and shivering on the closet floor with nothing but a washcloth to keep him warm?

Ornella pushes aside her empty glass and leans forward in a way that emphasizes her awe-inspiring cleavage. "You're quiet," she says, and she caresses the ring of his left nostril with her pinkie finger. "Ask anything. I'm an open book."

"All right," Chess says. "What does the name Ornella mean?"

"Mmm," she says. "It's Italian. It means a flowering ash tree."

On the word *tree*, Ornella slips her pinkie through the outer ring of his nostril, into his nasal passage. Which feels abrasive but good. And, for a fleeting moment, Chess wonders if there might be a market for nasal lubricant. Nasal massage oil, he'd call it. Or nose lube. Health food stores could carry it. But what would differentiate nasal massage oil from non-nasal massage oil? Ornella's finger thrusts too deep into his nose. Alarms shriek in his brain. His whole body buzzes, even his crotch—in fact, his crotch vibrates so hard it hurts. He pulls back, dislodging Ornella's finger and nearly tipping his chair in the process. He clutches at his groin. But the buzz isn't in his crotch. It's in his pants pocket. It's the pager the hostess gave him. A table for two is ready.

....

As Chess follows Ornella's car to her apartment, he texts Priti: "New girl not working out. Come to apartment at midnight or I send pics to ur mom." He's going to ditch Ornella as quickly as he can. But her bizarre living room distracts him. It has sky-blue walls with pastel-pink clouds. She flips a switch, and track lights with pink- tinted bulbs go from dim to ever-so-slightly bright. A huge woman materializes on the far wall, above the sofa. The face seems familiar. Ah yes, she's Dolly Parton. Or, rather, she's an airbrushed portrait of the face and bust of Dolly Parton. The image rises a full five feet from her breasts to the tiptop of her puffy yellow hair. Dolly winks at Chess with a glimmer in her eye. The collar of her rhinestone blouse has fallen open. This reminds him of Ornella's cleavage—which he suspects is the point. It's all so conventionally yet quirkily erotic that he finds it uncanny. Instead of excusing himself to leave, he takes out his last cigarette.

"Bum me one?" Ornella says.

He sets it in her mouth and lights it.

"So," he says, "you like Dolly Parton?"

"I'm obsessed," she says.

She tosses her coat over a chair and presses a button on the stereo. Dolly Parton's voice rolls in on a wave of banjos and slide guitars. Ornella invites him to sit beneath Dolly's massive breasts. The room could pass for an exotic fish tank, murky and blue and bubbling with greatest hits. He leans back as Ornella unbuttons his shirt. He holds his breath as she kisses his nostrils. He hates this. No, wait, he likes it. No. Help. He's drowning.

....

Twenty-six hours later, his lips and nostrils are as sore as hell, but he hasn't thought of Priti since about twenty-five and a half hours ago. This gives him the urge to text her to declare he has forgotten her. Then he remembers he said he would meet her at the apartment on Friday night. His stomach churns at the thought of losing Priti forever. He lies in bed with Ornella but feels like he's falling. He falls and falls, and there's no splash. Just a plume of smoke from Ornella's lips as headlights sweep the cottage-cheese ceiling. He wants to ask Ornella what it's like to live so close to a K-mart, who was her last boyfriend, how many boyfriends has she had, how many girlfriends, what kinks she's into besides nostril play, etc. And he wants to tell her about the Master of Submission, and about his mother who died in a tour-bus crash in Poland, and about Priti's propensity for bathing in a latex hood. But where to start?

"Do you believe in God?" he asks.

For a long time, it's quiet. Ornella's eyes stay shut. She is asleep. Chess pinches the burning cigarette from her fingers and stubs it out. Her ashtray has a logo printed on it: DOLLYWOOD. He presses his ear to the pillow and, all night long, dreams he's crawling across a field of bubblegum-scented breasts.

....

On Monday morning, sixty hours after Chess took his last Asinil, his nose aches as if someone has stapled it to his face. He flips Ornella's omelet and adds three slices of Swiss cheese, the way she says she likes it. He carries both plates to the breakfast nook, where Ornella sits with a towel around her torso. Her hair is up in another towel, turban-style.

"Let's go," she says. "Let's just go."

"Go where?"

"To Dollywood."

"Today?"

"No," she says. "Like in a week or two. Maybe next month?"

His omelet feels cold, so he eats it with his fingers. "What's with this Dolly Parton obsession, anyway?"

"She's Dolly," Ornella says and sets her fork on her plate. "She's an icon. She represents how life can turn out good, like when you've come so far from humble beginnings and now you get pretty much whatever you want."

"Your own amusement park, even," he says.

Ornella shrugs. "Do you like her music? I mean, honestly?"

A sharp pain jabs his nose, spreads across his face, and burrows back into his skull. "Ouch," he says.

"No pressure." Ornella pokes at her omelet. "Some days I can hardly stand to hear Dolly, myself."

"No," he says. "It's my skull. My nostrils, too."

Ornella tips his head toward the light. "Oh my god, Chess, your nose is raw. You need a doctor."

"No," he says.

"Why not?"

"He'll prescribe something to bring down the swelling, and you won't want me anymore."

Ornella puts her arms around his shoulders. "Of course I will, Mr. Sexynose." She kisses his cheek.

"But my nostrils," he says. "They're usually a lot smaller."

She shuts her eyes. "It's fine," she says. "Make an appointment."

"I wouldn't mind going."

"Good," she says.

"No," he says. "I mean, to Dollywood. I wouldn't mind going, someday."

Under the table, Ornella's toes slide up his shin, into his pant leg, all the way to his kneecap.

"Can I take naked pictures of you?" he asks.

"No fucking way," she says. And she laughs.

....

At a stoplight on his way to the doctor's office, Chess texts Priti: "Sorry I missed u Friday. I will delete all pics."

"Too late," she texts seconds later, "I deleted them and destroyed ur backup discs. And smashed ur hard drive."

Chess swerves his car to avoid slamming into a fire hydrant. No way. She is bluffing. Sure, she is hot-tempered, but he has never known her to destroy property. Did she take him seriously about posting the pics online? He would never do that. He just wants her so badly, wants her with him, wants her to hurt him. Clearly if she believes he could post those pics online then she does not know him at all. Not at all. She never did. What a bitch. He feels used. He was nothing but a vessel for her aggression. He will show her. He will punish her. Oh dear god, what has he become?

"There is intense swelling in your nasal musculature," Dr. K says. He steps back and reaches into his pocket, unwraps a lozenge, and pops it into his mouth. "Let's take care of that." He scratches his chin and prescribes 200 milligrams of Bewilderol three times daily.

"Can you prescribe something for my emotional state?" Chess asks.

"Which is what exactly?" Dr K asks.

"I have no self control and I want to run screaming out of my own skin."

"No," Dr. K says, "I have nothing for that, but this will stop the nostril pain and bring down your swelling."

"Co-pay, fifty dollars," says Dr. K's receptionist.

"That'll be $26.73," says the pharmacy lady with the elegant hair bun. No chopsticks today. Chess hands her a twenty and a ten. She counts out $3.27 from the drawer and places it in his palm. Chess nods and tries not to look at her as he walks away. But, at the end of the hair products aisle, he spots her reflection in one of those round mirrors that supposedly deter shoplifters. She's watching him. He grabs his crotch and blows her a kiss. She reaches for the phone, and he runs through the automatic doors.

In the car, he washes down a Bewilderol with raspberry soda. Driving to his apartment, he pictures himself on a roller coaster zipping up and down an immense steel replica of Dolly Parton's breasts. Priti was always so flat-chested, no wonder she hated strippers. But why the fascination with strip clubs? She would drag him along, but what for? To watch the dancers stumble, to comment on how they dressed, and to watch him watch them. Afterward, when they got home, Priti would pull out the straps and handcuffs, the whips and paddles, the ball gag and hangman's mask. And Chess would comply. Always comply. Always but once, that is. One night, he turned the tables. He threw Priti down and strapped her to the bed. "I don't think I like it," she said, and this killed everything. This smashed the looking glass and soured the milk. Priti did not object to his aggression. She didn't even cry. She just went cold and yellow and started shaking. He released her within a few seconds, and she curled into a fetal position. He spread a sheet over her, slept on the sofa, checked on her often, and made her breakfast. Then he put his faith in the healing power of saying nothing. For a month, they had no sex. So he invented the Master of Submission. When he assembled it and showed it to Priti, her jealousy knew no bounds. And that's when she agreed to let him take pictures.

....

Sure enough, Chess finds his apartment ransacked. Cushions, sheets, and clothes have been tossed everywhere. The hard drive is gone from the desk. The flash drive is gone from the medicine cabinet. All five backup CD's have vanished from their hiding spots. Yet the Master of Submission is still locked away in its case, in the closet, intact. This is a relief. But Priti came home. She walked through these very rooms once again. She even touched his shirts and underwear. And Chess wasn't there.

He claws at his cheeks. He has never felt so bereft.

He pulls out his phone, texts a polite greeting to Priti's ultra-conservative Hindu mother, and attaches a snapshot of Priti in a black bustier and a strap-on dildo, snarling at the camera—just a little something stored on his phone.

....

On his lunch break, Chess takes a seat at *Cafe Lieu-de-Travail* in the lobby. The elevator dings, and Ornella steps out. Her purple dress has a high neckline that covers her cleavage—a tragic loss—but the dress makes her waist look thin—a net gain. She walks toward him but slows as she gets closer. She sits and forces a smile.

"Your nose," she says. "It's tiny."

"I know. The doc gave me anti-swelling stuff."

"How strange," she says. "I wish you had texted me with a warning. God. I feel like such a bitch right now."

"Thanks for the weekend," he says. "It was fun."

"Yeah," she says. "It was."

"You should steer clear of me," he says. "I'm trouble."

"Oh. Wow. All right."

They nibble their scones and listen to the murmur and squeak that passes for silence in the lobby. Ornella takes his hand then drops it a moment later to sip from her coffee. After a while, she scurries back to her office.

Chess spends the afternoon with his head on his desk, chewing his cuticles, waiting for Priti to text or call or show up at the office, screaming.

But it's Ornella who calls.

"I'm so sorry," she says. "I think I love you, Chess."

He leans back in his chair. From his cubicle, he can see through the clear glass wall of the conference room, out the windows, and into a forest of mirrored buildings against a tableau of distant mountains. A hawk flies past with a silver fish clutched in its talons.

....

In the car on the way to the grocery store, everything goes gray. Chess's hand on the steering wheel goes gray. The red-and-white Safeway sign goes gray. Even the rainbow-colored bears marching stupidly across the bumper of the car he parks behind are gray. He tells himself, *Forget Priti. That flat-chested freak — what the crap does she mean to me? Why did I ever give a crap about her?*

And sure enough, when he gets out of the car, Priti's there. She does not see him. And she does not look upset. She's walking through the parking lot, holding hands with some guy. The guy looks Indian. Ah, so that's what all of this is about. It's racial. The Indian guy's collarless linen shirt hangs to his knees. His Indian pants are white. He holds a sack with a pineapple in one hand and, in his other, he holds Priti's hand. Plus, he sports an actual mustache. It's thin, the kind that would look sleazy on Chess but looks suave and ethnic on this guy.

Chess ducks back into his car as they walk past. Priti doesn't seem to notice him.

He picks up his phone and texts her: "I c u in the parking lot."

She looks at her phone, stops, and turns around. She spots his car instantly.

Ten seconds later he gets a text: "FUCK OFF!!!"

"U owe me $60," he texts.

"What for?"

"Last months utilities."

The mustache guy reaches into his shirt and pulls out a hemp wallet that hangs from a piece of twine around his neck. He walks over and slips a hundred dollar bill under Chess's windshield wiper. "Keep the change," he shouts. "Prick."

Chess gets another text from Priti: "Get a therapist."

"I need a top," he texts. "U r the ideal top."

"U top from the bottom," she replies. "And u r the worst bottom imaginable."

"I sent a pic to ur mom," he texts.

Priti stares at her phone for a minute. Then she glares at Chess and slowly shakes her head. Then she turns away, calls someone, hangs up, and hurls her phone at his car. The phone hits the windshield and smashes into pieces. Priti crumples to the asphalt, and the Indian guy bends over and puts his arms around her. A gray pickup driven by a gray lady backs out; and when it drives away, Priti and her Indian boyfriend are shutting the gray doors of a gray sedan. Sitting there, watching them pull out and roll away, Chess waves. He wants to get in that car with them and lie down, handcuffed, in the back seat. But he's here, in his car, in a parking lot, clutching his phone.

As he walks into the store, his nose goes numb.

....

Ornella cuts gray cheddar slices with Priti's old gray knife on the gray cutting board formerly known as Priti's, atop the counter where he first convinced Priti to punish him for being naughty. Ornella does not know these things are Priti's things. She does not know the countertop's history. How could she know anything about any of this when Chess hasn't even mentioned Priti — much less the former dungeon of his bedroom or the Master of Submission packed away in the closet. Chess beats a bowl of gray eggs with a whisk. His hands tremble.

"You want to fly or drive?" Ornella asks.

"Huh?"

"To Dollywood," she says. "Remember?"

"Oh yeah."

"Well, fly or drive?" She sets the knife on the counter. "Is that enough cheese?"

A ringing starts in his ears, softly at first. He looks at Ornella. She seems oblivious to the sound. This is the fourth new symptom in under an hour, after shaky hands, a numb nose, and a world gone gray. Could be the Bewilderol. Could be the Priti encounter. Could be anything. Chess knocks the pepper grinder on the floor. He adds too much salt to the eggs. He drops a tomato slice between the drip pan and the electric heating coil. He can barely grip the spatula, much less flip an omelet.

"You look awful," Ornella says.

"Uh," he says. "Um. Urgh."

He goes to the balcony for a cigarette — the balcony where he and Priti once slow-danced by candlelight, with fat cigars in their mouths and anal probes in their asses. Gray leaves wheel through the gray air. The breeze is warm. Down below, a gray dog sniffs gray bushes. Chess fights an urge to climb onto the rail and dive headfirst into the sidewalk. He can picture his head smacking the cement. His skull cracks. His spine snaps. His body flops the wrong way over. And his insides spill like a sack of rotten fruit. But he's on the second floor, not high enough to do real damage.

He shuts his eyes and inhales. *In with the poison, out with the love.* It's over with Priti, he tells himself. He has Ornella now. For now. He doesn't deserve her. She will leave him in the end. Or sooner than the end. And that's his problem in love: whatever and wherever the end is, he does not know how to get there. The odor of greasy beef drifts by from the burger joint on the corner. He feels hungry yet not hungry. The entire bloody universe has conspired to make him let go of Priti. And he can't.

"I burnt the omelets," Ornella says, leaning through the gap in the sliding door, looking gorgeous. "They're black and crunchy."

"I have to show you something," he says, and he leads her into the bedroom. He sits her down on the edge of his bed and reaches into the closet. In less than a minute, the Master of Submission stands fully assembled.

"What the hell is it?" she asks.

"It's a self-contained bondage and submission device."

"I've never heard of such a thing," she says.

"I invented it."

She presses a knuckle to her lips.

"With this," he says, "a person can experience the degrading thrill of submission, without a dominant partner. Of course, if one is available, there's no rule that says a dominant partner can't participate."

Ornella stands and walks around the device, touching its straps and testing the sturdiness of the secondary crossbar. She does not seem repulsed. Then again, she does not look turned on, either. Chess wants to crawl into the device and fall asleep for a week.

"So," Ornella says, "when you get into it, you're the slave and it's the master?"

"Yeah, sort of. You're the bottom, so to speak, and with this you don't need a top."

"Cool," she says and kisses his cheek. "Bottoms and tops aren't my thing, I guess, but I bet a lot of people would buy this. You should license it and market it, or whatever."

Chess feels so much relief that he suddenly wants to marry Ornella. He bites his lip. "I'm still working out a few kinks," he says. "So to speak." He leads her back to the balcony and wraps his arms around her shoulders. She leans against him, and they watch the sunset.

"We should go," he says.

"For dinner? Good. I'm starving."

"No," he says, "to Dollywood. I mean it. Right now. Let's go."

"Oh come on. It's twelve hundred miles away."

The glass in the sliding door beside them reflects gray elm trees and the gray park across the street. A gray leaf blows onto Ornella's black hair and quivers there for a moment before it floats away.

"Come on," she says. "Don't mess with me. Let's order take-out. You want Chinese, Mexican, or seafood?"

"I want Dollywood," he says.

She turns in his arms. Her thumbs rub circles in the hollows behind his collarbone. He could be the worst person on the face of the planet, but in this moment his heart overflows. With what? With compassion. He should probably spare Ornella the misery of knowing him. He should tell her to run before it's too late. But she looks so shy and content now, and she feels so soft. And maybe this time his luck will change. Or maybe he will. He nods, yes and yes and yes.

Seagulls

She asked how seagulls recognize each other, how they know friends from strangers. This was near the end. We had driven from Denver to Santa Cruz—a journey long enough to make us hate each other for a few hours. After forty-five minutes at the shark-attack museum, we spread our towels on the sand.

"I mean," she said, "do gulls recognize their mates as they're both stabbing after the same dead fish?"

"I'm not sure," I said.

With her finger, she drew two short lines curving to a point in the sand, then two more, and so on, until the beach between us ached with hungry stick birds.

The Fractured Museum of Us

1.

My father swore he would never permit my mother to own a dog, but old age made that an impossible promise to keep. The day after doctors confined Dad to a wheelchair, following his fourth knee surgery, Mom rescued a miniature dachshund from a highway median. The dachshund had golden brown fur and no tags. She named him Herbert.

"Keep that damn dog the hell out of the bedroom," Dad told her, "or I'll whack the fucker."

And Dad kept that promise. He whacked Herbert with a newspaper every chance he got, until tumors, ulcers, and painkillers made memories of even Dad's smallest motions. The last time I visited, Dad slept all day. When I opened the bedroom door to say goodbye, Herbert trotted in, hopped onto the bed, and scratched a nest into the blankets between Dad's legs. For several minutes I watched them—Dad and Herbert—as they drifted through waves of sleep.

2.

Gray cubicle. File folders. Fluorescent lights. Vacation snapshots. I was playing solitaire on my lunch break when the phone beeped. I answered: "Systems, this is Mark."

A breathy, feminine voice spoke. It was my brother Ron.

"Mom just called," he said. "She's hysterical."

"Hey, you." I shut my eyes. "It's been a long time. How's life? I thought Mom disowned you again."

"She couldn't find your work number. It's an emergency."

I cupped my hand over my ear to block out the noise of the office.

"So, what's up?" I asked.

"It's Dad. He's gone."

I heard nothing after that.

3.

I stand by the sliding glass door and look at Dad's toolshed. Dad's boat. Dad's gas grill. Dad's shovel. The scent of toast floats in from the kitchen. A magpie lands on Dad's overturned wheelbarrow. The sky looks as gray as the fleshy underside of Dad's chin during the service the day before. Herbert, the dachshund, has gone missing.

Mom comes in with a coffee mug. She wears her hair in a bun. Sofa springs chirp and coffee sloshes onto her pink nightgown as she sits.

"I'm so tired of crying," she says and blows on her coffee. After a while, she pulls half a piece of buttered toast from her bathrobe pocket.

The doorbell rings. Mom leans forward. I hold up a hand and tell her I'll answer the door.

"It's your father," she says. She sits back and nibbles her toast. "I dreamt this would happen. He's come to apologize."

I go to the door. It's the neighbor, a retired plumber. His muddy fingers clutch the tube of Herbert's body. Herbert thrusts himself into my arms and flicks his tongue at my lips.

"Herbie dug a hole under the fence," the man says, pointing at the garage. "Little rascal came to sniff at my ducks."

"Thanks," I say. "His name is Herbert."

"Ah, Herbert. Right." The man licks his lip. "My wife and I were so sorry to hear about the loss of your father. Retired Navy, right?"

"Army."

"Good man, good man."

"Was he?" I ask. "That remains an open question."

The neighbor lifts his cap and pats his comb-over. I thank him and shut the door.

4.

A photo of my mother, my brother, and me, taken when I was six years old, hangs in the hallway between the bathroom and the living room. The picture shows Ron and me standing on either side of a tire swing. Mom's legs dangle through the tire, and her arms hug it. She smiles. Ron smiles. I smile. I wear corduroy pants and a flannel shirt over a T-shirt. Ron, who must be nine, wears jeans and a leather pilot's jacket with a fuzzy collar. The sleeves are too short for his arms. Leaves gather in the grass. The sun spills in and shines on the left sides of our faces. The right sides hide in shadows.

5.

On the day of the funeral, Ron came to his door in a peach-colored blouse, a black sweater, a long black skirt, black pantyhose, sensible black pumps, and hoop earrings.

"Come in," he said. "Lemonade? Iced tea?"

"We're late."

"Shit, I'll grab my purse."

He vanished down the hall, leaving me in the living room with his mauve sofa, his floral wallpaper, his love beads, and half a dozen Chinese-food cartons and soy sauce packets on a faux-marble coffee table. Several potted plants, with leaves so green they had to be silk, hung from the ceiling in macramé slings.

"Let's go, Ron," I said.

He came back with a finger to his lips. "I am not Ron anymore, and you know it."

The trailer park was still deserted as we walked to the car. "So, let me get this straight," I said. "Your neighbors don't know your name is Ron?"

"They don't," he whispered. "I'm Geraldine."

"Seriously? I told you to switch to something that does not have a man's name embedded right there in it. That's all anyone's ever going to hear, you know?"

Ron smacked my shoulder with his purse. I opened the passenger door for him, and he slung the purse into the back seat. The strap caught on the head rest.

"I honestly don't care," he said.

Neither of us spoke again until we pulled out of the trailer park.

"So, what do the neighbors call you?" I asked.

"They don't." He fluffed his hair. "No one talks to anyone. How's Mom?"

"Devastated," I said. I flipped the turn signal and pulled onto the highway.

Ron stared out the window. "Foolish, foolish woman," he said.

North of Pueblo, we drove past box stores and across the prairie toward Colorado Springs. Thunderheads piled up behind the mountains. Wind blew hard, making it tough for hawks to cling to their fence posts. At half past ten, I eased off the gas so we wouldn't arrive too early.

"I have to ask you something." I said.

"Yeah?"

"Do you still hate Dad?"

Ron leaned back against the head rest. "Right now? Today? I guess not."

"Oh," I said. "Wow. I'm surprised."

Ron put his hand over mine on the gearshift. "Maybe you'll feel better when it rains."

"Why? Do I look distraught?"

"Yes," he said. "But rain makes everything better."

I shook off his fingers and gripped the steering wheel with both hands.

6.

(Fourth of July, 1978)

I sprinted out of the house into the back yard. Dad stood on the patio, whistling "Oklahoma!" and bending over the grill. Mom was stretched out on a lawn chair with her nose in the *Encyclopedia of Supernatural Events*. I leaped over a sack of fireworks by the picnic table and juked around the grill.

"Mom," I said, "you ain't gonna believe this."

She adjusted her pink sunglasses to the crown of her head. "Don't say ain't."

Dad picked up a Nerf football from the grass and spiraled it at my leg. It hit just above the knee. I rubbed my thigh and said, "Ronnie's doing something in the basement." A bottle rocket whined through the sky. "When can we light fireworks?"

"After dark, babe. What's Ronnie doing in the basement?"

"Come see."

She brushed bangs from my eyes. "Just tell me."

Dad swatted the grill with his spatula and said, "Goddammit!"

Mom shot a smile at him. "Oh hit it again, Jack. That'll light it."

Dad went to the shed.

"Well, what's he doing?" Mom asked.

"It's a girl thing."

"I'm a girl so you can tell me. And stand up straight."

She pushed back my shoulders and gave my cheek a soft smack.

"Come see," I said.

Mom raised her eyebrows at me. "You've always got to stir the poop, don't you?"

"Not always," I said.

When she stood, the backs of her legs had a crisscross imprint from the lawn chair's woven straps. I followed her into the house.

"Go quiet, Mom."

She slipped out of her rubber-soled sandals. "Quiet as a mouse, babe."

Holding her hand, I brought her down the steps far enough to peek into the basement. We kept an orange carpet down there. An olive-green sofa faced the corner, where our black-and-white TV was showing a rerun of *Gilligan's Island.* On the screen, Mary Ann begged a cannibal to set her and Ginger free. Three feet from the TV, my thirteen-year-old brother begged too. He had an American flag wrapped around his hips for a skirt and one of Mom's white blouses knotted at his belly. And he moved as Mary Ann did. She shrugged, he shrugged. She waved her hands in the air, and he did too.

We watched him until a Kool-Aid commercial started, then she dropped my hand and went downstairs.

"Ronald," she said, "what on Earth?"

Ron spun. Mom slapped his cheek much harder than she had patted mine.

"Where did you get that flag?" she said.

He held his face. "From a box."

Mom stepped back and looked at the ceiling. Ron peeled the flag from around his waist. Underneath, he wore cut-off jeans.

Mom took the flag and folded it. "This is the flag from Uncle Stephen's funeral."

"I didn't know," Ron said.

"Don't I-didn't-know me, Ronald. Where did you get that blouse?"

"It was in the laundry basket."

"I've seen a lot of things in my day," she said, "but I've never—and I mean never—seen anything like this."

Ron unbuttoned the blouse.

From my perch on the stairs, I said, "You ain't a girl."

Ron told me to shut up, and he handed the blouse to Mom. He was so skinny his ribs showed.

"Ronnie," Mom said, "why in the world would you dress like that?"

"Next time, be Gilligan," I said.

"Marky," he said, "if you don't shut up—"

Mom's voice drowned out his: "Go to your room now, before I get half a mind to tell your father. This would make him sick. Just sick."

Ron marched up the stairs. As he passed me, he whispered, "Thanks a lot, you pinhead snitch."

I shoved him. He punched my shoulder. My mouth opened and no words came out, just a pathetic squeak.

"Dammit, Ronnie! You will not, under any circumstances, strike your brother again for as long as you live. Do you understand me?"

Dad came to the top of the stairs. "What the hell is going on down there?" he said.

"Mark is a tattletale," said Ron. "And I didn't do anything wrong."

Dad looked at me. "Is that true? Did you tattle on your brother? Answer me now. Because you know that's not how we settle things around here." He came down three steps and lifted me by my arm. "You look at me when I talk to you, mister."

"Calm down, Jack," Mom said.

"I'm trying to teach him something, Evelyn."

"Well don't."

"Why not?"

"Just leave Mark alone. Ronnie was wearing your brother's flag as a skirt."

Dad looked at Ron, then at Mom. He let go of me.

She told him everything. When she finished, Dad came down the steps and jabbed two fingers into Ron's throat. Ron doubled over and fell to the floor.

"Your uncle died for that flag," Dad said.

He grabbed Ron's hair and told me and Mom to go upstairs. Mom took my wrist and dragged me out to the yard. Ron cried as Dad slammed the basement door behind us.

Standing in the back yard, listening to my father's shouts under the whine of a thousand bottle rockets, I lit a sparkler. Its white light flashed on Mom's face. She looked at me as if she didn't know me.

7.

In the tire-swing picture, Ron's mouth hangs open. It's not slack, though. He's shouting something. The trace of a smile lingers on his lips. He desperately wants the attention of the man holding the camera.

Our dad considered himself an ace photographer, a collector of small joys and important moments. But his collection could not have held many such moments—certainly not enough to fill a museum, unless that museum were a narrow, twelve-foot hall connecting a living room to a bathroom and a couple of bedroom doors. And the key artifacts in this museum, if its collection were taken as a whole, would look like so many strange transformations, so many tense mornings, so many long drives and sleepless nights with stars whirling overhead.

Now, when I look at these photos and the half-smiles caught forever on our faces, the images rise up and fill me with something unexpected. With love. And with light.

8.

As we pulled into a parking spot outside the funeral home, fat drops splattered the windshield. Ron turned to the window, and pressed his nose to the glass. I checked my watch: four minutes until the service.

"Mom's flipping out right about now," I said.

"Good."

Rivulets ran down the windshield and made shadows on the dashboard.

I reached into the glove box and grabbed my whisky flask. It fit nicely in my jacket pocket. I cut the engine and put a hand on Ron's padded shoulder. "Ready for the big show, Geraldine?" He flashed his teeth, touched his lipstick. "Ready as I'll ever be." I have to admit that Ron was agile in heels. He jumped a mud puddle and beat me to the door. But when he peered into the kite-shaped window, he jerked back as if the glass had shocked his nose.

Mom's face hovered there.

I nudged Ron aside and pulled open the door. Mom stood with her arms locked over her breasts. Her nose was red. She wore a black scarf over her hair. Organ music wafted out and mingled with the patter of rain.

"You brought him here, looking like this?" she asked.

I wiped water from my face, put my hand to my heart, and felt the pleasant curve of the flask.

9.
(Spring 1984)

I was cutting my scrambled eggs and sausage links with a fork when Mom reached across the table. She yanked Ron's hair. He twisted free and said, "Ow!"

"What?" I said. "What was that about? What happened?"

Mom crossed her arms. "Ask your brother."

"What was that for?"

"None of your business," he said.

He was seventeen. I was fourteen. By then, we had established a code. The way he told me this was none of my business meant he would make it my business when he told me about it later.

The waitress came over. "More coffee?"

"No, thank you," Mom said. "I'd be tempted to throw it in my son's face."

The waitress shook her head and went behind the counter to fill ketchup bottles.

I tugged Ron's plastic bracelets.

"Butt out, frogface," he said.

Mom slapped the table. "That's it. You two, get in the car."

I shoveled a huge bite into my mouth before Ron pushed me from the booth. We went to the parking lot to wait by the station wagon. Ron chucked pebbles at the highway ramp. I watched Mom hand the waitress cash and wait for change. The plate-glass window reflected the sky over our neighborhood, cloudless and pale blue. Mom looked genuinely happy in there now, paying for breakfast. When she came out, her smile vanished. She jammed her key into the car door.

"Ron," she said, "you watch your mouth at the doctor's or I will tell your father."

"Tell him what?"

"About your crush."

Ron didn't speak another word as we drove, and neither did I. We didn't have to. We both knew the question was "Who?" and the answer was "Greg Louganis."

10.

I stepped into the foyer of the mortuary and leaned close to Mom's face. "Give him a break for once," I said.

"I'll break his goddamn neck," she said.

Ron looked at the awning overhead. "I'll just wait in the car."

"War's over, gang," I said. I leaned against the polyester drapes. They reeked of embalming fluid. "Hey, Mom, I like that scarf. It's perfect. Where'd you get it?"

Mom raised an eyebrow. "Carolyn loaned it."

"It's just right," I said. "Is everyone here?"

"Everyone but you two." Her cheeks turned as red as her nose. I put a hand on her neck, and the softness of her skin startled me. She pushed my hand aside and said, "Today, of all days, you two should pay him some respect. That's all."

"OK," I said, "but I'm not setting foot in there without Ron."
She wiped her forehead. Then she stepped out the door, wrapped her arms around Ron, and hugged him for several seconds. I reached for the flask. Mom pulled back and patted Ron's cheek. Ron flinched then moved in for another hug. This one lasted until I screwed the cap back on the flask and cleared my throat.

57

II.

Grampa Al died the day Ron went to college. After that, Dad tried hard for three weeks to be good to me and Mom. He took us out for dinner, bought a new TV, invited me to a football game. He even let me drive most of the way to Minnesota to scatter his father's ashes in the headwaters of the Mississippi.

I parked the Dodge in an empty dirt lot. A cool, dry breeze blew through the area. Dad leaned back into the car to offer a hand for Mom, but she stayed in her seat.

"It's too cold," she said. She opened a magazine in her lap and leafed through the pages. "I'll wait here."

Down by the water, the breeze stirred cattails. Dad picked up a stick from the path and tossed it into the weeds. Trees swayed against the sky where Grampa Al had pissed out the window of a small plane some fifty years ago—or so he used to tell us.

"Al used to fish here," Dad said. He stepped into the water. "Let's have a moment of silence." He bowed his head.

With one foot in the river and one in the mud, I pictured Grampa Al's head, his white hair so short it prickled like pine needles, his pink scalp dotted with freckles. He used to wear gray-brown socks the color of wood left in the rain. Dad took a plastic pouch from the mortuary box. He cut the pouch with his buck knife then held the pouch high. He tipped it over and let the ashes fall through the air. What was left of Grampa Al clouded the water around Dad's ankles.

Dad waved his hand to take in the river, the clouds, the trees. "And so," he said, "Al will be forever in the water, now."

I imagined Grampa Al blending into and becoming the water, steadily flowing down to the ocean. Soon he would rise up and rain down on us again. I pictured him in a plane, overhead, pissing on all of this. I let my fingers trail through the murky water.

12.

A firing squad shot rifles at the sky. Crows scattered from the trees. Mom nodded and sobbed. The sky opened itself and drained everything it had. Fifteen people made it to the cemetery, including the hearse driver and the minister, but, as the rain picked up, the people dispersed with the crows.

Ron and Mom waited in the car while I stood at the foot of the grave. I turned up my collar, tucked my glasses into my coat pocket, and let the rain soak me. For no good reason, I sang the national anthem. The cemetery workers looked up from the truck where they waited for us to go away so they could do their jobs. In an hour, Dad's hole in the ground would be just a scar of freshly turned dirt in a field of sod and marble slabs. So I sang louder. My car engine rumbled. Ron had scooted behind the wheel. He waved for me to hurry. Mom waited in the backseat with her face in her hands. Somewhere a bell rang. Then another. Church bells and thunder, rain and the rocket's red glare. I sang for a long time, proving to no one but myself that our flag was still there.

13.

With the dachshund in my arms, I stand before the photo of Mom and Ron and me with the tire swing. Herbert squirms into a comfortable position, straddling my forearm, and rests his nose in the crook of my elbow.

I lean closer to the image. Herbert sniffs the glass. I set him down, and he runs up the hall to the living room, where Mom sits with her coffee and waits for her dead husband to come home. I take down the picture frame and carry it to the kitchen table. The cardboard back slides out, and there it is—the white sheet with our photo on the other side. Without turning it over, I tear the page in half. I tear the halves in half then tear again.

Ron comes in—no makeup, his long hair a mess. If he weren't wearing one of Mom's bathrobes, he'd look like a bricklayer or a butcher. He rubs his eyes then pours a cup of coffee. I shuffle pieces of the photo and tear the last of the eighths into sixteenths. Ron pulls up a chair and looks at what I've done. Piece by piece, he turns over the puzzle: my arm, Mom's legs, his jacket. He slides the pieces back together.

"Aw," he says, "I liked this one, Frogface." He touches the corner where Mom's ear is severed from the rest of her head. "She was so pretty."

Mom stands in the doorway, with Herbert at her ankles. She watches us move around the pieces of that picture. I expect her to shriek or cry or rush for Scotch tape, but she says nothing and sort of smiles.

Eight Years Later

Her face hovers above his. She digs her fingernails into his shoulders. Her toothpaste breath makes a pillow of air on his cheeks. "Listen," she whispers. Moonlight angles through the window onto her face. "I have a thought."

He kisses her.

"At dinner," she says, "your friend said every cell in the human body gets replaced every seven years, right?"

He puts a finger to her lips.

She pulls away. "Every cell, right?"

He glances at the clock. It's 3:28.

She pulls his face toward hers. A car hisses past on the street below. She asks again: "Every single cell?"

"Yeah," he says. "I think it's kind of an urban myth."

"But is it true?"

"I think so."

"You think it's true or you know it's true?"

"Let's say it's true. Every single cell."

She lifts her nightgown over her head and tosses it off the bed. This is the first time he has seen her breasts since—god, since Calgary.

"I'm twenty-four," she says.

"I know," he says. "I don't get it."

"I was fifteen last time it happened."

"Last time what happened?"

She peels off his boxers and straddles his hips. Out the window, a plane crosses through the Big Dipper. The trees, heavy with wet leaves, billow over the house next door. "My father," she says. "It's been eight years." She slides forward and lifts off, brushing her body over his. "Eight years. Now there's not a single cell in my body that he ever touched. Not one."

Plantlife

Dear Rabbi Cahan,

My name is Monah Feldberger. We met in Chicago twenty-three years ago, during the week of my husband Alvin's funeral. You came to my house and patronized me for fifteen minutes, praising me for what a devoted widow I would be to my husband. Honestly, moments after I met you, I began to hate you. But our conversation soon turned to gardening, and we talked flowers and plants the rest of the afternoon. To this day, you remain the one person I have met who knows more about soil enrichment than I do. So please, Rabbi, bear me out here. I need your advice.

I live alone now, far from Chicago, in a cabin near Green Mountain Falls, Colorado. Yesterday while Oreo, my Chihuahua, and I were on the back patio, the sun passed behind a cloud. A breeze jingled the wind chimes, and one of my tomato plants reached through the air to caress another. Then the second plant caressed the first. Yes, Rabbi, my tomato plants caressed each other — and not as if the breeze had blown them together. Oh no. They gently stroked one another's leaves. Then they bent inward, untied themselves from their stakes, and leaned together in a fluid motion. And they hugged. This nearly gave me an aneurism.

You know as well as anyone, Rabbi, that plants are alive. They turn their leaves and flowers to the light. Like us, they grow, they age, and they die. So, with rich soil, plenty of love, and just the right amount of sun, I ask you, why couldn't a few plants start to move a little more freely? And it wasn't just my tomatoes. As they fondled each other's flowers, my larch branches waved in arcs that had nothing to do with wind. The lilac bush pushed against the ground and lifted its roots from the dirt then shuffled across the lawn. My sunflowers danced with the maple saplings poking through the grass. And the grass! The blades of grass, themselves, milled about the yard like very tall ants.

Little Oreo spun circles of joy, but he did not bark. In fact, he did not so much as step off the porch. Later in the afternoon, I found one of his tiny deposits on the living-room carpet. But I'm getting ahead. After about fifteen minutes of this craziness in the yard, I went inside and checked the TV to see if maybe vegetation had come to life everywhere. I mean, who knows? Though there was nothing on CNN, my houseplants were playing hide-and-seek in the living room. At first they scooted their pots around on the parquet floor, and soon enough they pulled free of the dirt and pattered through the house on their roots.

I went to the kitchen for a sandwich. Thankfully, my bell peppers and cucumbers were not doing anything unmentionable in the crisper drawer. I ate my sandwich at the table and wondered if the plants even knew I was here. As if it could read my mind, my big rubber plant stepped up behind me and wrapped its branches around my shoulders. One leaf patted my head. I froze for fear the plant would strangle me. But she didn't. In fact, she held me in a gentle, slightly prickly cuddle that lasted several seconds, and I felt a kind of inner warmth I have not known since before my husband Alvin's death. Not that Alvin was a particularly warm human being, Rabbi. Frankly, he was often as cold as a dead fish. Anyhow, when I scooted around in my chair to return the embrace, the rubber plant waddled out the back door.

My place sits at the far end of a dirt road, Rabbi. I get no traffic. The neighbors' places are vacation cottages owned by families from Kansas. So here I was, completely alone with a houseful of sentient, mobile plants. Naturally, I went for the phone. I wasn't sure who to call, so I dialed 9-1-1. The plants grew very still. They cocked their leaves as if to listen. When an operator answered, I mumbled something about a wrong number and hung up. The plants went back to tracking dirt on my carpet and rearranging my furniture. The ridiculous Venus Fly Trap my son sent for my birthday leapt around the room with its traps snapping. The way the Venus clattered up the drapes and shimmied across the curtain rod, that poor moth didn't stand a chance.

Each time I picked up the phone, my plants stopped to listen, so I was careful. I had a mundane conversation with my sister Thelma in Boca Raton, then a humdrum talk with my old nursing buddy Bev. I did not mention the plants to either of them. Celia, my lovely, young daughter, picked up the phone once I promised her machine I had not called to nag; but the very instant I mentioned the rubber plant—which had been Celia's back in college, when she did not care for other living things unless they drove sports cars—all the houseplants grew quite still and tense. The rubber plant leaned toward me for a moment and gestured for the other plants to stay calm. I told Celia the plant was fine then changed the subject.

When I hung up, the tension passed. The rubber plant walked down the hall. The other plants seemed harmless again and entirely uninterested in me. My carrots skittered away from the garden when I wanted to cook a soup, but the tomato vines actually delivered their ripest fruits to the kitchen. I took this to mean I could eat the fruit but not the plants. As my soup cooked, I formulated a plan. After dinner I would walk to the car, get behind the wheel, and drive away as fast as I could.

It was dusk when I turned the key in the ignition. I shifted into reverse and looked over my shoulder. Two maple trees stepped behind the car. When I turned to go across the yard, the foxtail pine hopped in front of my car. Rabbi, I doubt you've seen a *Pinus balfouriana* grin, but I can tell you it's almost creepy enough to make an old woman lose control of her bladder. Almost.

I got out of the car, but the trees stood still. As I turned to walk to the road, a coyote began to cry in the woods. The cry was squelched mid-howl. I heard a yelp. Then crunching metal and glass. As I spun around, those trees smashed and folded my car to the size of a suitcase. One perfectly good Saturn, gone. I went to the edge of the yard, but a maple branch kept me from going farther. The plants next door looked normal enough. They did not dance or hop or hug. The world had changed only on my property, it seemed. I stood there for a long time, trying to figure out how I'd gotten into this mess. Was it something in the fertilizer? Was my cabin built with radioactive bricks? The sun fell behind the mountain. I shivered. Because the plants wouldn't let me leave and didn't want to hurt me, I went back inside.

What I found in my living room—well, Rabbi, it was weird. The plants had knocked every remotely religious item (not that I have many) from my walls and shelves. (I admit, I am not active at the local synagogue. Why not? Mostly because arrogant, young Rabbi Faigelman is a fool who compliments every old woman's hair every time he sees us, no matter how bad we look.) Anyhow, my handmade glass mezuzahs were shattered on the living room floor. The plants had swept the shards of colored glass into a swirl of geometric shapes that spiraled out from a green, leafy-looking thing at the center. The effect was a cross between a Tibetan sand mandala and a flowery china plate. Also, the plants had ripped my late husband Alvin's prayer shawl to shreds and hung them from the ceiling like falling snow. The tin Star of David from the wall above the fireplace was now bent into the shape of—of what?—some kind of pagan seed or maybe a nut. Clearly, these were not Jewish plants.

They seemed happy to see me return, though. My rubber plant (which I had nursed from near-death ten years ago, after Celia left it in her hot car for three hours) shuffled over with a glass of fresh-squeezed lemonade. I sat on the sofa and sniffed the lemonade. It smelled fine. I drank it. My spider plant crawled up the wall and tucked itself in the space between the ceiling and the books on my top shelf. The African violets climbed one upon another and switched on the TV for me. Still nothing on CNN about plants, so I clicked over to *Sex and the City*. My eyelids were heavy. I felt drowsy. Only too late did I realize the lemonade had been laced with valerian and a hint of chamomile.

I dreamt of my husband Alvin. In the dream he had hair. He was buried up to the knees in a large clay pot next to a stream that flowed through the yard. I held a watering can. I wanted to get across the stream to water Alvin, but I saw no bridge. The only way across was to walk on the back of a large snake. I hate snakes. So I waved at Alvin, and he waved at me. I tossed him a fertilizer stick and fell back into the warm embrace of my rubber plant. That is all I remember.

I awoke this morning in my bed. Early sunshine poured through the windows, which was odd because a tall fir tree had always blocked out the light there. The house was silent. I sat up. Nothing moved. Not a plant in sight. Oreo wasn't in my bed. I called, but he did not come. Still dressed in yesterday's clothes, I walked to the living room.

The furniture was gone. My sofa. My end tables. My TV. Everything. Gone. The plants had spread six inches of top soil across the floor. At the far end of the room, where my TV once stood, an altar had been fashioned on a large boulder. Don't ask where the boulder came from, Rabbi, because I couldn't tell you. A golden-green moss was draped over the boulder and gave the room a warm, yellow glow, which was nice. On top of the boulder, the plants had placed a pagan nut or seed icon fashioned from my Star of David.

The plants, and I mean hundreds of them, filled the room and stood perfectly still. They seemed to be worshipping the nut/seed thingamajig. Or maybe they were meditating. I don't know. The smallest plants—violets, carrots, etc.—knelt close to the altar, while the larger plants stayed farther back, in order of height. The room had a palpable, humid energy—very still, very alive. The only plant that moved was the Venus Fly Trap. It crept behind me as I tiptoed to the kitchen. I don't know what it had been eating, but the Venus had grown ten times larger. Now it was the size of an eight-year-old with a healthy appetite.

I went into the kitchen and shut the door. The linoleum floor was still bare, though dirt trails crossed the room here and there. For reasons I could not guess, my gas stove had been disconnected and moved to the center of the room. I opened the refrigerator and took out a carton of milk. As I reached to the cupboard for a glass, something moved in the back yard. Through the window, I saw trees pacing back and forth, guarding the property line like soldiers on patrol. The carton slipped from my hand and milk gurgled into the sink. I picked up the phone. The line was dead.

By now, my little Oreo should have been skittering at my feet, ready for his breakfast. I stepped onto the back deck and called. Oreo did not come. The trees paused a moment in their pacing then kept marching the perimeter. I am a worrier by nature, Rabbi, but this was unnerving. I walked back through the kitchen to search for Oreo among the plants, but the Venus Fly Trap blocked the door to the living room. I hadn't heard the Venus come in. And, unless I am mistaken, it glared at me with the unmistakable arrogance of a predator. Its traps clicked open and shut. They now gaped to the size of a bear's mouth. Yet one of the traps remained closed. Something wiggled inside it. A short, black, fuzzy tail poked out between the trap's teeth.

I lunged for the stove, forgetting it was disconnected. The Venus chuckled—or it seemed to, Rabbi, but it's difficult to read the body language of plants—as I flipped the burners on high. No flame. I went to my utility drawer, but the matches were gone. The weed killer I kept under the sink had vanished.

That Venus nodded its traps, clickety-clack, and shifted its weight toward me. I clenched my fists. The Venus snorted. I pulled out my big drawer of baking trays. There, under the trays, I found my old butcher knife in a cardboard box the plants had apparently overlooked. I held up the knife and let the blade glimmer in the daylight.

When I turned around the Venus lunged and punched me hard in the belly. I buckled to the floor. My shoulder crashed on the linoleum, but I held onto that knife.

The Venus thrust a trap at my head, but I was ready and hacked at the branch. The trap fell to the floor. Then another lunge and another chop. The Venus's amputated branches flailed, and I kicked it across the room.

I stood up. "Give me the dog," I said, "and I'll let you live."

The topmost of the Venus traps shook from side to side. I came closer. As the plant retreated toward the living room, I swung the knife and, kerchunk, I chopped through that Venus's stem and separated it from its roots.

The Venus toppled and scrambled for the door.

I reached for the stem and caught it just above the first branch. The Venus grasped at the doorknob and opened it a few inches. For one second, while that door gaped on a roomful of plants engaged in a solemn religious ceremony, I thought I was doomed: they would find out I'd attacked one of their own, and they would probably kill me in return.

But a branch from the rubber plant shoved the door shut.

I hacked again at the Venus's stem. Its traps gasped. What was left of the Venus shuddered, drooled, and went limp in my hand. I pried open the trap that held Oreo. My poor little guy was all sticky and as sad as could be, but he perked up when I poured him a bowl of kibble.

I filleted the Venus's stems, diced its leaves, and removed the teeth from its traps. Then I cut the traps into thin slices, which I marinated in walnut oil and soy sauce. I wrapped the rest in plastic wrap, sealed that in a Tupperware, and stuffed the corpse into my freezer.

When I came out of the kitchen, the nut/seed worship was over. Most of the plants had gone outside. The rubber plant was there still, dusting the altar. As I walked toward her, butcher knife in hand, she froze. A few other plants made a quick move to stop me, but the rubber plant waved them away. She waddled closer, held open a leaf first, then extended a whole branch. I dropped the knife to the floor. Slowly, serenely, the rubber plant opened her branches. I leaned forward. She caressed my cheek. I collapsed into her limbs. What can I say, Rabbi? The strangeness of all this had gotten to me. I wept, and the rubber plant patted my shoulder and ran her leaves through my hair. After a good, long cry I stood up and brushed myself off. The knife was gone. The other plants went about their business. The house felt strangely at peace. I kissed the rubber plant. She lifted my nightgown up, over my head, took my hand, and led me down the hall to the shower.

And that was this morning. I made two more halfhearted attempts to leave the property this afternoon, but the trees would not let me go past the mailbox. Since I sat down at the kitchen table to write this letter, the plants have shown no interest in me at all. I only hope they will permit me to place this in the mailbox. If all goes well, this should reach you by the end of the week. As I said, Rabbi, I need your advice. And here is my question, which pertains to *kashrut* rules about plants. Clearly, land animals that eat other animals are not kosher. But tell me, please, are there grounds to suggest that a carnivorous plant would be non-kosher? Assuming the plant is edible and tastes good, and all the needles have been removed from its traps, may I eat it with a clear conscience?

Thank you for your time, Rabbi Cahan. I anxiously await your reply. Please give my regards to your poor, lovely wife.

Sincerely,
Monah Feldberger

The Suicidal Juggler

Kathleen went for a stroll in the park with Tom. They took a slow lap around the pond, then drifted over to the playground. The sun came out, and leaves quivered in the sky. Children occupied the swings, so Tom and Kathleen walked to a green picnic table off to the side. People had carved initials and obscenities on every inch of the table and its benches. Tom and Kathleen sat with their arms around each other and watched the toddlers orbit their mothers.

"I love kids," Tom said. "Just love 'em." His hand felt damp. His Adam's apple pulsed as he spoke. His breath smelled faintly of blueberry donut. "Hey, check out this guy."

Kathleen looked around. "Who?"

"Him, right there."

Tom pointed at a tall man in green denim overalls and a red thermal shirt. The man wore a bowler hat and stood on an open patch of grass, with a pyramid-shaped stack of baseballs at his feet. He picked up a ball, turned it in his hand, then threw it at the sky. As the ball shot toward the clouds, slowed, and dropped, the man planted his feet and crossed his arms. He waited with a smile, staring straight ahead. The ball hit the grass with a thud, inches from his feet.

Kathleen gasped.

The man gave a clownish shrug and picked up another ball. After looking it over, he hurled it into the air. Again, he folded his arms and waited for the ball to strike. It fell behind him.

"What an idiot," Tom said.

He massaged Kathleen's hands, fingers, and wrists, as she watched ball after ball pound the grass near the man's feet. One ball grazed his arm. He lifted his hat, mimed wiping his brow, and gave the same comical shrug.

Kathleen brushed away a tear with the sleeve of her sweater. Tom cleared his throat. "This city is full of freaks," he said.

He took her hand and led her back to her apartment, where they had sex again on the living room floor. She liked the way he held her down, but it hurt when he put his hands around her neck. She told him to stop. He kissed her eyelids when he said goodbye. Snow fell all afternoon. White beads clicked and melted on the window. After three days, the snow stood two feet deep. After ten, Tom still had not come for the blue jacket he left draped over the back of a kitchen chair.

Endangered Species

Two weeks after my brother Travis sawed open his wrist with a steak knife, I sat beside him in the car on the road home from Breckenridge. He slept, I drove. His snores gave the ride a faltering rhythm. Though younger than I, he weighed thirty pounds more. His eyebrows were thick, his nose clammy and flat. His mouth drooped open. His head lolled into the space between our seats, and a pink scar peeked like the slit of an eye from under his sleeve.

"You're a coward," I whispered.

Snowflakes blurred past the windshield, and the vents dumped hot air on our boots.

"You're a waste of flesh," I said in full voice. "You're a stupid, awkward, shuffling, ungrateful pile of crap, with big feet."

He snored.

"Face it," I said. "You are a fag."

Yet another breath spurted through his hairy nostrils. I put a hand on his shoulder and shoved him toward the far window.

"Sweet dreams," I said.

"Pussy," he said and fell back to sleep with a smile.

Travis and I had not spoken on the drive up. We didn't talk much on the slopes, either, and he went unconscious the minute we climbed back into the car. I had no idea why my parents thought this trip would somehow help Travis save Travis from himself. Yet Dad had insisted we drive to Breckenridge, for old time's sake—as if Travis and I had made the trip more than once. "Get him to work this out," Dad said. "We'd rather have a gay son than a dead son," Mom added. Apparently the wrist-cutting had gotten their attention.

West of Florissant, we passed a bison in the sunset. The beast stood thirty feet from the highway, and its hulking body was an ink stain on the endless white of the valley.

I remember when my father's fingers wrapped around my leg and shook. "Wake up," he whispered. The station wagon rested. Dad's hand moved to Travis's leg, which dangled beside mine, over the back seat. "Wake up," Dad whispered again. "Look at the buffalo?" I saw only Dad's headrest and, above that, Mom's eyes in the rearview mirror. "Look," she said. I undid my seat belt. Travis groaned, and Dad's voice went deeper: "Travis, sit up and look." Travis grabbed a toy car from between us and hurled it at Mom. I stood on my seat, and my cowboy hat bumped the ceiling. There must have been two hundred bison in the herd in front of us — massive brown piles of fur and hooves glistening in the sun, shambling across a road that cut through a meadow. Travis grunted. "Final warning, Travis," Dad said. Travis undid his safety belt and Dad lifted him into the front seat. "What are those?" Travis asked. "Buffalo," Dad said. Travis bounced and pointed. "Buffaloes! Buffaloes! Can I pet one?" Dad laughed. "No, you may not pet a buffalo," said Mom. "They're dangerous." Travis reached for the door handle. "I wanna touch a buffalo!" "No, honey, I'm sorry." "But I wanna!" Dad smacked Travis's hand, and Travis howled. Mom took him onto her lap and hugged him as he whimpered. Dad said nothing. I sang "Row, Row, Row Your Boat" until the last buffalo lumbered over the road.

....

The Subaru pitched down then thudded up onto the road. I gripped the wheel. Travis huffed into consciousness. "Jesus fucking Christ," he said. "What the hell was that?"

I looked back but couldn't tell. Miles of highway and snow filled the rearview mirror.

"We're fine," I said.

Travis rifled through his coat for a cigarette. "Was a moose napping in the road or what?"

"It was a pothole."

He pushed in the lighter. I pulled it back out.

"Not while I'm driving," I said.

He pushed it in again and fiddled with the radio, found only static from one end of the dial to the other. He shifted in his seat to face me.

"So," I said. "You got a girlfriend?"

"Me? Not right now. You?"

"I do."

He pushed it in again and fiddled with the radio, found only static from one end of the dial to the other. He shifted in his seat to face me.

"So," I said. "You got a girlfriend?"

"Me? Not right now. You?"

"I do."

He slapped the dashboard. "Breaking news! How long?"

"Since October."

"Ooh, long term." He fingered a crack in the dashboard. "You do her yet?"

I cleared my throat.

"Well, have you fucked her?"

"Don't be crude," I said.

"Oh come on, gay-wad." He reached for the lighter and lit a cigarette. "Does she do the nasty with you or what?"

"I never kiss and tell," I said. "Why don't you have a girlfriend?"

Travis snorted. "High school girls," he said. "They're fucking insane."

"How would you know if you never date them?" I asked.

"Believe me, bro," he said, "I know."

"But if you never go out with—"

"Fuck off," he said. "There's a pizza joint in Florissant."

I switched on the headlights. The snowflakes looked fatter in the light, and the road shimmered.

....

Florissant had little more than a filling station, a motel, a convenience store, and a couple dozen trailer homes. Back in 1969, President Nixon designated a nearby field of petrified tree stumps as a national monument: the Florissant Fossil Beds. In turn, some clever entrepreneur called his pizza place Stumpy's. We sat at a red Formica table. The waitress slid menus from between the napkin dispenser and cheese shaker. As she leaned across the table, Travis took a whiff of her perfume.

"Sweet ass on her," he said as she walked away.

"Didn't notice," I said.

An old man at the bar—the only other person in the place—swiveled on his stool to face us. A ridge of skin ran down his cheek. He pointed a finger at me and said, "Bullshit."

"Pardon me, sir?" I said.

He shook his head. "How could you not notice that ass?"

The old man spun back to the bar. Travis reached across the table and flicked my chin with his finger. I pushed his hand away. He blew his nose into a paper napkin, and I took a napkin too, put it in my lap, and watched the snow fall.

....

I remember the tail end of our Black Hills trip, after we saw the bison herd. That evening, we lugged our bags into a shabby Motel 6 on the edge of Rapid City and crossed the street to eat at Shakey's Pizza Parlor. Travis and I stared through a big window onto the kitchen while Dad placed our order. A chef sprinkled cheese and dealt pepperoni slices as if they were playing cards. Travis pointed at the back of the kitchen. Another chef had slipped his hand up a waitress's skirt. She jerked away and dropped a tray of mugs. Root beer, cola, and ice nuggets splashed onto the floor. The chef laughed as the waitress pushed his arm away. An older man, probably a manager, came into the room and scolded the waitress. She dropped to her knees and collected the mugs. The chef came to the window where we stood, picked up a ball of dough, and tossed it overhead. As it spun in the air, he gave us a wink. Then Mom called us over to sing "Camptown Ladies" with Ye Olde Time Piano and Banjo Combo. Dad's mustache was white with beer froth.

....

The Stumpy's waitress had brown eyes and short, dark hair. We ordered a large sausage and olive pizza, two house salads, and, for Travis, a plate of fried cheese sticks.

"Can you rush that?" said Travis. "It's an all-night drive."

The waitress nodded and went to the kitchen.

"Did you see that smile?" he said. "She wants me."

"No she doesn't," I said, "and you've got nothing to prove to me."

"I'm telling you."

"What she wants is bigger tips to take home to her husband and kids," I said.

Travis leaned back in his seat. "No way, I give off the right hormones." He tapped a cigarette from his pack.

"Pheromones," I said.

"What?"

"You give off pheromones."

The old man at the bar made a small, formal bow in his seat as the waitress delivered his chicken sandwich. She grinned at him and put her elbows on the bar. Her smile was cute and lopsided and dipped toward her left shoulder. They spoke quietly as he picked onion slices from his mayonnaise.

Travis sprinkled salt into his water and drank the whole glass.

"So tell me," I said, "if the waitress were a gay dude, would you take him out back and kick his ass?"

Travis sneered. "I would if he looked at me wrong."

"And how's that?"

"Fuck you," he said. "What are you getting at?"

"I'm getting at you," I said. "You were expelled from school, and I want to know why you're picking fights."

"I am what I am, bro," Travis said. He entwined his fingers and stretched his arms toward the ceiling. "Have you given the hot beef injection to your girlfriend yet?"

"Chill out," I said.

The waitress set the cheese sticks on the table. "There you go, gentlemen," she said, and she carried off our soda glasses for refills.

"She doesn't want you," I said.

"Fuck you she doesn't," Travis said. "Watch and learn."

He arched his eyebrows and called for the waitress.

"Everything OK?" she said as she set down our sodas.

"Just fine," said Travis. To prove his point, he dipped a cheese stick into tomato sauce, stuffed the whole piece into his mouth, and stared at her as he chewed. She walked away. Travis held up his left hand. "See? No ring."

I sipped my root beer. "She's too old for you."

"No such thing."

"You don't have to prove anything to me," I said.

Travis stuffed another cheese stick into his mouth. "I bet anything I can do her."

"*Do* her?"

"Get laid, dude. Right there." He pointed at a neon sign across the road. It showed a green-and-yellow Native American warrior in a headdress. Beneath his feet, orange words flashed one at a time, then all together: HAPPY HUNTING GROUNDS LODGE.

I dipped his last cheese stick into the sauce. "No chance, *dude*."

"Look," Travis said. "Here's my terms. If the waitress agrees to meet me at the lodge, you have to tell me if you've porked your little college chick. If the waitress dogs me, I shut up for the whole drive home. Deal?"

"Either way," I said, "we drive home."

"What?"

"Even if she agrees to meet you, which she won't—but just in case she does—you ditch her and we drive home."

He dragged from his cigarette. "It's all about the thrill of the hunt," he said.

I checked my watch. "5:45. You've got twenty minutes."

He pulled his shirtsleeves down over his wrist. "No sweat."

"So," I said, "why'd you do it?"

"Do what?"

"Cut your wrist."

His head dropped for a moment. He glanced at the old man at the bar, then out the window, then back at the table. "Don't go there," he said.

I slurped the last of my root beer.

The waitress brought our pizza and salads. We ate in silence. Travis reached for the Parmesan shaker with his left hand, winced, and put it down. "I'm not supposed to lift anything heavier than a kitten," he said. Then, with his right hand, he smothered the pizza with Parmesan, salt, and red pepper flakes. When he had finished his half of the pizza, one of my pieces, several cheese sticks, and his salad, he went to the cash register, where the waitress was counting coins.

The old man finished his sandwich, dropped a five-dollar bill on the counter, and put on a suede hat with earflaps. As he pushed open the door, the waitress said, "Goodnight, Mr. Greer." He waved and walked past the Happy Hunting Grounds Lodge. My watch said 6:05. I slipped two dollars under the pizza tray.

Travis and the waitress stood by the register, talking. I jingled the car keys and handed the waitress our bill. She rang it up, and I paid. Travis winked at me. "Sorry I left that book at home," he told the waitress. "It would rock your world."

"Sounds interesting," she said. She played with a bracelet on her wrist. Her tongue slid over her lips for a split second, and she smiled. Her eyes made me want to call off the bet. She was actually into him.

Travis looked at me, then at the door, then back at her. "Guess we'll go check in," he said, gesturing to the lodge across the road. "You should stop by later."

She shifted back on her heels. Her chin rose an inch or two. "I thought you were driving all night."

"We changed our minds." Travis pulled at my sleeve. I shrugged. He moved closer to the counter. "Guys change their minds too, you know. Come over after work?"

She leaned forward and softened her voice. "Just say what you want, Travis."

"Honestly?" he asked.

She nodded.

He grinned at me, then back at her. "I want to get into your pants."

"I've got one asshole in there already," she said. "What would I do with another one?"

She wiped the counter with a wet rag. Travis grabbed the keys from my hand and went out the door. A blast of cold air blew into the restaurant. I pulled out a five-dollar bill and tossed it onto the counter.

The waitress folded it and slipped it into her pocket.

"Come back soon," she said.

Fresh powder covered the parking lot. I wiped the windshield with my sleeve then got in. Travis had the engine running. I sank in beside him and watched snow until my breath fogged the window. As we pulled onto the highway, Travis muttered, "Bitch."

About a mile out of town, beyond the last few trailer homes, a thump shook the car. Travis hammered the brakes. We skidded to a stop. The engine cut off and a warning bell chimed. Travis covered his face with his hands. "Please god oh fuck oh Christ," he said.

The wiper blades swiped back and forth.

I put a hand on Travis's arm. He was shaking.

"Oh god," said Travis. "A person was back there. In the road. I don't fucking know what just fucking happened."

The rear window had frosted over. I opened the door and got out. In the red glow of the tail lights, I could see a gray mound slumped across the gravel shoulder a few yards back. I zipped my coat and walked toward the mound. It was a man in a gray coat. The old man from Stumpy's. His arms lay limp at his sides. His hat covered his eyes. The furry earflaps glistened with snow. I touched his leg. He coughed and sputtered.

"Sir," I said, "can you hear me?"

The car door flew open and Travis dropped to his knees on the gravel beside the old man. The man moved his lips like a suckling kitten. Travis clutched the gray coat and whispered, "Thank fucking God." The sight of them—Travis cowering and cursing, the old man gulping air—set off a strange, floating feeling in my body. I stood there on the verge of hysterical laughter, until it hit me: Travis could go to jail for this.

He wiped his nose with his glove. "Should we take him back to Florissant?"

"No hospital there," I said.

"Then let's call a fucking ambulance."

"He'll die waiting."

Travis patted the old man's coat. "We can't move him."

"If we don't get him into the car," I said, "he'll freeze to death."

"But moving him could kill him."

"Fine," I said. "You want to go ask that waitress for a phone?"

Travis stared back toward Florissant and shook his head.

I bent over the old man. "You'll be OK, sir. We are going to get you into our car."

I took the legs and Travis lifted the shoulders. The old man wasn't heavy. Snowflakes pelted our faces as we moved to the car. We set the man down as gently as we could, opened the hatchback, and lifted the man about six inches until Travis's bad left hand lost its grip. The old man's skull slammed the pavement and his jaw thudded against his chest. Travis stood there, clutching his wrist.

"Pick him up, idiot," I said.

"Shut the fuck up," Travis said.

I grabbed his ski jacket with both hands, spun him around, and slammed him against the car's rear gate. He tried to push my hands away, but I wouldn't let go. His head thumped against the window a couple times, and his whole body went limp.

"God dammit, Travis, help me get this guy into the fucking car!"

Travis shut his eyes. I breathed on his face. I felt like I was looking at myself in the mirror with my eyes shut.

The old man moaned.

"Sir," I said, "we're taking you to a hospital."

He kept moaning.

"Let's do it," Travis said.

I stepped back. Travis opened the hatch and shoved aside the skis. I took the old man's shoulders this time, and Travis lifted his legs. We set the old man in place and wrapped him in a dirty blanket. I drove. Travis faced the back, clasped his hands around the man's shoulders, and mumbled prayers. The old man coughed a few times, then fell silent.

Travis pivoted in his seat. "You think I'm a faggot," he said. "So that's what Mom and Dad think, isn't it—that I can't face up to being a fag? My life is so fucking pathetic." He gave a low, eerie chuckle.

"What's funny?" I asked.

"You," he said. "I know you don't think I'm anything like you, but I'm even less like you than you think."

Travis punched my shoulder. I laughed, but it wasn't an easy laugh. Snowflakes drifted through the low beams then shot past the windshield like stars. We rode those last twenty miles down the pass, chuckling and cursing, as the old man's lungs filled with blood.

The Zen Master's Fish

One day a Zen Master of the Fukui monastery tossed a fishing line into a river. A young monk approached, bowed, and said, "Zen Master, the nature of the river is both transient and eternal. We cast a line into the river then we pull the line out of another river. How then, can we say that we 'catch' a fish? Does it not catch us?"

"Ah," the Zen Master said. "You fail to grasp that the river's impermanence is eternal."

The monk scratched his head. "What does this mean, that the river's impermanence is eternal?"

The Zen Master reeled in the line. At the end of it, a fish flopped around with a hook through its lip. The Zen Master removed the hook from the fish's lip and held up the fish by its tail.

"Listen," the Zen Master said. "This fish swam all its life in a single river. When I fish, I fish in countless rivers. Yet the river, the fish, and I are one."

The monk stared.

The Zen Master ran his bony finger along the fishing wire. "You see, this is the line that connects us."

The monk scratched his cheek.

The Zen Master waved a hand back and forth between the fish and the bamboo pole. "This is the line that connects the fleeting to the everlasting and the everlasting to the fleeting."

The baffled monk inhaled and tried to smile.

"Whoop whoop whoop, whoop!" said the Zen Master, and he knocked the monk's chin with an elbow. He jabbed two fingers into the monk's eyes and swatted the monk's nose back and forth then gave the monk's bald head a wet slap with the fish. And the Zen Master pulled a wooden mallet from his basket and hammered the monk's forehead ninety-nine times.

The monk blinked, and for a moment a light gleamed in his eyes. He bowed to the Zen Master with respect and gratitude. The Zen Master reciprocated the bow, picked up the fish, and dropped it into his basket.

The fish gasped for water and got only air. Then the fish gasped again and again and again and again and again and again and one more time, then again, then once more.

The End of Norway

Neal, a self-described hell-raiser from several of Boise's finest kitchens, came to Paris for a three-month intensive residency at an elite culinary academy. He had promised his wife the trip would mark an end to his wild years and a transition into life as a family man. But, on the day of his flight home, Neal bought cheese and a bottle of burgundy and checked into a hostel. That night, he hugged his knees and watched his phone flicker and buzz on top of his duffel bag. He drained the bottle one sip at a time and chucked the phone through the open window at dawn. The display flashed again as the phone left his fingers. It landed on a debris pile in the far corner of the construction site next door. He got dressed, went downstairs, and swung a leg over the corrugated metal fence. Two Moroccans in hard hats yelled at him. Neal dropped to the sidewalk, checked out of the hostel, and took a room in a business-class hotel near the Louvre, where he stayed four nights until room service informed him that his Discover Card was declined.

From Paris, he headed northeast. A week in Bruges, three days in Amsterdam—he refused to stay long enough for a place to lose its shine. When the MasterCard finally dried up, he rented a studio on the fifth floor of a rat-hole tenement in Copenhagen and stayed seven weeks. On Sundays he would go to the library and delete emails, unread, from his wife, sister, and mother-in-law. One subject line used the phrases "third trimester" and "bed rest." This made Neal's head hurt, so he quit his job bussing tables at the Indian Taj and hopped a cheap flight from Copenhagen to Oslo. There, he swapped his last 330 euro for a couple thousand kroners, bought a whisky flask, tucked it into his jacket pocket, and took a train to the fjords. He planned to ride until the kroners or the trains ran out, whichever happened first. His goal: to get stranded as close as possible to the Y at the end of N O R W A Y on the map, or farther still, up beyond the Arctic Circle.

Two hours outside of Oslo, the train burst from a tunnel above the Hallingdal River. The water lay flat and reflected every crevice of the mountain then shattered on rocks and split around a tree-bristled island. Green pines gave way to grays and browns that reminded Neal of home. He lurched up the aisle to the toilet, where he heaved what little he had in his stomach then rinsed his mouth with a swig from the flask. Back in his seat, he pressed his forehead to the cold window. Patches of snow nestled among the rocks, and a veil of frost slowly covered the windows. Neal gripped his armrest and strained against the glass. The train blasted into another tunnel and, three minutes later, broke free in a misty valley of fairytale villages and tall trees. All of this scenery washed over Neal and whirled him into a state akin to ecstasy. But in the afternoon he grew bored and got off the train at Voss.

Neal shoved his duffel into a locker. He downed two cups of train-station coffee fortified with whisky then bought bread and a two-day-old *International Herald Tribune*. The grocer's teenage son gave Neal directions to a trail that cut through a valley of waterfalls and streams.

The valley was gorgeous. Snowcapped trees dripped in the sun. A mile out of town, Neal couldn't hear a car or a plane, not a single machine, nothing but water and wind. He left the trail for a patch of sunlight near a fringe of ice on the riverbank. A burst of ice tumbled from a tree across the river. He kicked off his boots and sat cross-legged on a bed of leaves. Five feet beyond his toes, a ribbed steel pole poked through the surface of the river. The tip was painted fluorescent orange. Without coffee and sugar, the whisky felt sharp. He sprinkled the last few drops into the mud, screwed on the cap, and unfolded the newspaper.

After a while, a lime-green minivan creaked to a stop on a bridge a hundred yards or so downstream. Neal hadn't spotted the bridge, and for a moment the minivan appeared to hover above the water. A man got out and looked in Neal's direction for a good thirty seconds.

He pulled something from his van then walked across the bridge and disappeared behind the trees. Soon footsteps crackled through the woods. Neal pulled on his boots, stood, and turned.

The man came over a ridge. He wore a brown coat, a blue knit cap, and rubber waders that covered his knees. He was older than Neal, around forty. Brown curls poked from his knit cap. He clutched a two-foot-long steel pipe in his right hand.

Neal saluted, then shrugged, then waved. He was ready to punch hard and run if this guy tried to hit him with the pipe. The man stopped ten feet away and nodded. He had gray eyes. His fingers gripped and released the pipe. He said something in Norwegian.

"Sorry," Neal said. "Speak English?"

"A little," the man said.

"Is this your land?" Neal asked.

The man glanced over his shoulder, toward the trail. "This part belongs to Holst. Who are you?"

Neal said he was a tourist. He had stopped to rest and was about to head back to Voss. As he spoke, the Norwegian hefted his pipe. Neal held his palms forward and forced a smile. The man lowered the pipe and said, "Oh, no, this is not for you."

Neal extended the flask as a peace offering, forgetting it was empty, but the Norwegian waved it off.

"You are an American?" he said.

"Sure," Neal said. "Hell yes, I am."

The man chuckled. "OK, I show you something." He walked past Neal, stepped into the water, and peered at the orange-tipped pole. Neal could have walked away, but he stayed. The man reached into the water, tugged on a chain at the base of the pole, and lifted up the stiff, dripping carcass of a muskrat. He tossed it onto the leaves at Neal's feet. Water splashed on Neal's boots. The muskrat's upper lip was curled, revealing gritted teeth. Its spine was frozen in an arc. Its thick tail curled like a snake in the leaves.

The Norwegian reached into his coat and pulled out what looked like a Bowie knife. Neal decided this might be a good time to haul his ass back to Voss, but he hesitated.

"This animal is worth maybe thirty kroner," the man said. "Pays for petrol, at least. I find most of my traps empty today." He used the knife to cut a root tangled in the chain then thrust his hand into the water and reset the trap.

Neal backed away from the muskrat.

The Norwegian pocketed his knife then pointed his pipe at Neal. "Stay," the man said. "Have a look at real Norway life. This is not a tourist thing." He kept an eye on Neal and waded a few steps downstream. He pointed at another pole about fifteen feet from the first. "Looks empty."

Neal asked where the Norwegian sold his muskrat fur.

"In Voss, in Bergen. There was a man in Myrdal, in the old shed where now they rent bicycles and canoes. He paid for skins, the most money." The Norwegian glanced over his shoulder. "Oh shit." He went around a small bend.

Neal followed. A black-and-white tail swished in the water near another orange-tipped pole.

"Shit," the man said again. "Damn it. I usually bring my gun for these, but I leave it in my truck when I see you down here. I do not want to scare you."

"Yes. Well, no," Neal said.

The man squinted at the sky. Neal stepped closer, to see past a bush. The tail belonged to a raccoon. She was treading water. Her right leg was caught. The chain gave her three feet to swim in a circle around the pole. As she swam, her black eyes stared at Neal.

"This one is worth 150 kroners," the man said, standing just beyond the raccoon's reach. "Fills the tank for a month."

"I thought raccoons were native to North America," Neal said.

"They come over here, maybe as pets, maybe on boats. I don't know."

The raccoon's eyes reminded Neal of a Ukrainian prostitute in Amsterdam. Moist eyes. Sad, enraged, bewildered.

"I'm going now," Neal said. "It was nice to meet you."

"No," the Norwegian said. "Just stay."

He reached for the steel pole. The raccoon snarled and lunged for his hand. He cocked his arm and slammed the steel pipe down on her skull. Her head slapped the water and sank. Her body twitched and flailed. Bubbles rolled from her mouth. Milky white spittle flowed from her lips. Neal stood still. The raccoon's underwater flailing slowed to a gentle wave.

The man walked farther downstream. "Ho," he said, "I catch a mink here." He reached for another trap and pulled another stiff, wet carcass from the mud. "Is it a damn cat? No, a mink. You must be delicate with these. The glands stink like a skunk, if you pop them."

The Norwegian tossed the mink to the shore and came back to unlatch the raccoon. He held her up by her broken leg. "Step away," he said and tossed the raccoon to the bank. She thudded onto her back, took two hoarse gasps, and stopped moving. Swollen, gray nipples poked through her fur. Her litter had probably drowned trying to stay with her. Neal looked around. The sky had begun to grow dark, far sooner than he would have guessed. He blinked to adjust his eyes to the shadows. He checked his watch. It was after eleven. If he ran now, he could easily make it to town before dark.

The Norwegian said he'd make almost three hundred kroners from these animals. He tossed his steel pipe onto the leaves beside the raccoon, turned his back on the riverbank, and bent to reset the trap that had held the mink. Neal picked up the pipe.

It felt cold and gritty as he turned it. For a moment, he thought he might puke, but he doubled over and nothing came up.

"I sometimes harvest ten thousand kroners in a month," the man said. "Not much, but it buys toys. Happy children make a happy wife, you know?"

Neal stepped to the edge of the water. When the Norwegian turned, he saw the pipe in Neal's hands.

"Are you going to hit me?" he asked. He laughed.

Neal didn't answer. The man stopped smiling. A muscle over his eye began to twitch. He reached into his coat. Neal thrust the pipe forward and the man put his hands in the air.

"What are you doing?" the Norwegian said.

When Neal didn't answer, the man muttered, "You don't want to hurt me. I work at a dairy farm in Myrdal. I have three children and a wife. My mother needs insulin."

"You're right," Neal said. "I don't want to hurt you."

"Just put away the pipe," the man said. "We can be friends. Why not? Come for dinner. We will laugh. Drink beers. My wife will make *krumkake.*" He wiped his hand across his cheeks. "Or maybe we go apart and never meet again. That would be fine too."

"Yes, it would," Neal said.

"Hey, do not go off the trail back to Voss." The man pointed at his brown jacket and Neal's dark green one and said, "We are fools. We should stay in town unless we dress in bright orange, glow-in-the-dark orange. It is hunting season. Hunters could be anywhere."

Neal didn't see anyone in the trees around them, but he thanked the Norwegian for his advice. "Now go," Neal said.

The Norwegian stepped out of the water, stuffed his carcasses into a canvas sack, and shuffled over the ridge.

"Kiss your wife when you get home," Neal said.

He tossed the pipe across the river.

On the trail back to Voss, Neal came across a doe and two fawns at the edge of the woods. They watched him. The doe's thigh muscles rippled in anticipation of a chase. Neal raised his arms and mimed a hunting rifle in his hands. He lined up the sight and squeezed the trigger. He imagined shaving the skin from her muscles, slicing her open, and gutting her. The whisky buzz grew lighter as he walked, and a breeze cleared his head. His jeans swished with each step. He could feel his heartbeat. He stopped on a wooden footbridge near town, fished into his pocket, and pulled out fifteen hundred kroners. Enough for a raccoon to buy her own pelt a dozen times over. Enough for a good knife and a winter coat, maybe a camp stove. Not enough for airfare to the States, though. Not even close.

Onion Ring

Dolores dips a napkin into her water glass and dabs the wet corner onto a spot of ketchup on her sweater. As she does this, I notice her finger — the one where the platinum band used to be.

"Don't be eccentric," she says. "I grind my teeth when you're eccentric. You know that."

She smiles her way through a club sandwich with fries on the side. When she's done, she tucks her bra strap under her sweater and says it:

"I met someone."

The tiny hairs on the back of her ringless ring finger have grown dark.

"We're really happy together," she says. "We met in Paris."

I sip my water and set the glass back on its circle of condensation.

Dolores tilts her head to the left. "He's great. It amazes us both, all that we had to go through to find each other."

I dip an onion ring in ketchup and smear red loops around my plate.

"Uh-oh," she says. Her eyes are full of whatever fills burnt hazel eyes when they try to express an emotionally correct blend of love, kindness, and resolute detachment. "Are you upset?"

I poke an onion ring at the Catalina dressing.

She reaches across the table and puts a hand on my water glass. "Are you crying?"

I fold the onion ring in half. The breading cracks at the creases. The whole thing fits into my mouth. It's salty.

"Oh my god," she says with a smile then a frown that puffs her lips. "I didn't think you felt that way anymore."

I lift my water glass to my mouth. Her hand retreats to her lap. As I drink the last few drops, a big clump of ice slides down to my nose. I hear teeth grinding — could be hers, could be mine, could be the toddler's in the next booth.

"I'm speechless," she tells me. "I guess right now you're going through what I went through eight months or a year ago."

The waiter refills our water glasses and smiles at Dolores, takes her plate, walks away. Dolores leans back against her bench. "You should find someone to talk to," she says. "You have to forgive yourself, and then you have to forgive me. Learn to love yourself. You and I, we had—" She shuts her eyes. "We had wildly different marriage acumens."

I dip another onion ring, a small one, in ketchup.

"I know it's hard," she says, "but if I made it through then you can, too."

I roll my eyes as if a fly were swirling around my head—a routine that always made Dolores laugh, back before she grew tired of me.

"You'll make it," she says through a clenched jaw. "You'll see."

I steady my gaze on the bridge of her nose and extend my hand, open, across the table. She reaches for me.

"Just let it all go," she says. "Know what I mean?"

I squeeze her hand, fold most of her fingers over her palm, and slide the onion ring around her ring finger. "I do," I say. "I totally do."

Our Lady of the Rockies

I meet a girl and her father on the crest of a hill. She waves as the dog and I climb, and the dog bolts so fast I think he might hit the hilltop and keep running into the clouds and on to the sun. I hold back a shout with a fist to my lips, and the dog skids to a stop and licks the girl's shoes. When I get close, the father juts his chin to greet me. With one hand, he blocks the wind from a camp stove. With the other, he flicks a silver Zippo. It sparks but won't light, and he tosses it to the dirt. His fingers are black with grease. "Always something," he says, and he reaches around to scratch his own back.

The girl rubs the dog's ears, and I ask her questions. She is twelve. She figure skates. She loves vampires and feels "discombobulated" by the leap from elementary to middle school. Her hands dance as she speaks of cell-phone coverage, her dead best friend, and a stainless-steel stud someone will punch through her eyebrow the day she turns eighteen. Her apple-yellow hair hangs in a thick braid down the back of her pink T-shirt.

"Knock it off already with the piercing talk," her father says.

I scope out the glen below. It looks empty, and I tell the father I will pitch my tent a bit downhill. He asks what I'm up to in the woods on a Wednesday. I say I got laid off, and he tells me to join the club.

"You remind me of a boy I know," I say to the girl. "A special boy."

She smiles then frowns and looks to her father. He examines his hands. I pick a burr from the dog's coat and feel an impulse to give the girl a gift. But I have only the dog, and he is not mine to give.

The father tips a canvas chair onto its side by the camp stove, grabs his lighter, and coaxes a blue flame from the burner. "Give me the coffee," he says, "and those sausages."

The girl pets the dog again.

"Hurry up," her father says.

She unzips a backpack, hands him a tin pot, and pulls out a plastic bag of ice water and a pack of eight sausages. The dog sniffs at her knees and crotch. I tug him away by the collar. The father asks if I have enough food. I point a thumb over my shoulder and turn so he can see the trout dangling from my pack. I tell the girl to stop by later if she wants to play fetch. She says she might. Her father tells me no offense but he won't let her visit a stranger in the woods. I say good call. And, as the dog and I hike downhill, the girl sings the same catchy pop song my son was humming as I drove him to the mall this morning—a song my wife has insisted Satan himself surely composed.

....

I make camp and dig a fire pit on the far side of the draw. The dog sniffs everything in sight while I fry the trout with wild onions and morel mushrooms. Whiffs of pork and garlic from the sausages on the hilltop swirl through the fir trees and mix with sage, trout, olive oil, smoke, and mist off the stream. I look around and breathe it all in. This is the first peace I have known in weeks.

I have come to the woods to escape drama at home. My wife and I have long suspected our son Peter is gay, and we have worked hard to come to terms with this. Erin wanted to take him to psychologists for counseling. I argued for loving the sinner even if we hated the sins he might someday commit. Our worst fear was that one day Peter would ask us to pay for surgery to make him our daughter. But the real shock came two months ago, when he sat us on the sofa to announce he would forgo gender altogether.

"I am not a boy," he told us, "and I am not a girl."

Erin's grip nearly broke my fingers. She asked Peter what the hell he was, then. He had a term for it:

"I am an asexual androgyne."

I put my arm around Erin's shoulders. She jerked away and asked Peter if he was some kind of sex robot. He said, "Oh my god," and she warned him never to use the Lord's name in vain. Meanwhile, the dog licked his paws.

"Sorry," Peter said, "but I won't let society dictate my identity or tell me what to desire."

"Have you joined some kind of cult?" Erin asked.

Peter stood up. "I don't expect you to understand," he said. "But I do expect you to love me as I am."

I felt strangely proud of my boy, or whatever he was, and it was pride—not judgment, not regret—that pushed a tear from my eye. Peter saw this, and he too started to cry. I reached for him, but Erin dropped to her knees and burst into prayer. She shouted at the ceiling with such force I expected her to conjure the wrath of God then and there. Peter's face crinkled. He ran from the room and took the stairs three at a time. His bedroom door did not slam, but it shut hard and the lock clicked. The dog came over and put his head in my lap. Erin turned to me.

"You have to put a stop to this," she said.

"How?"

"Pray on it. Read scripture. It's been a long time since I saw you with your Bible. Stop going through the motions. Consult Pastor Weaver. We're losing our son. Do something."

"I am," I said. "I'm letting him be."

Over the next few days, Erin made it clear she blamed me for Peter's strangeness. I had let him play with dolls. I had let him wear towels as skirts when she was not home. I had refused to spank him, and I had permitted him to listen to popular music. This androgyny business was just a clever smokescreen to hide his homosexuality, she said. If I hadn't kept her from intervening early on, maybe Peter could have been saved.

So she went after him hard. She grounded him indefinitely. Then she dragged him to Pastor Weaver, who knew a camp where they cured homosexuality. But the cure would cost three thousand dollars we did not have, so Erin opted to shout the gay out of Peter despite his repeated claims of wanting no sex at all.

"Where is your porn stash?" she said to him one night at dinner.

Peter squinted at her as if she were insane. "What porn stash?"

"I checked your browser history," she said.

"And?"

"No porn. You must have magazines or videos. Where do you hide them?"

Peter looked to me for help, but I felt paralyzed. My marriage was crumbling, and the thought of living without a wife or an income terrified me. I stared into my tuna casserole and waited for Peter's answer.

"I'm going for a walk," he said.

"Take the dog," I said.

"No."

A week into Erin's campaign of terror, we raced to the hospital so doctors could pump a black spatter of pills from Peter's stomach.

Afterward, while Peter slept, Erin wept onto my chest. I felt so angry that I could not bring myself to wrap my arms around her. I had never been a violent husband and had not raised my voice in years, but it took all my strength not to punch her in the face right there beside Peter's bed. I prayed that night for the first time in a long time, for more patience.

After three days in Crisis Watch and a month in the psych ward, Peter came home loaded with Zoloft and conviction. But Erin was ready. I begged her to take it easy on him, but she cut off his Internet access and declared her shame for what her son had become.

Then came three weeks of full-on Armageddon. The more Peter resisted, the harder Erin prayed. And the harder she prayed, the less I believed that God gave a damn. So I knocked on Peter's door. And I knocked again.

"What?" he said from within.

"Hey, Pete, how about you and I go camping, just like old times?"

"Is this some desperate, backwoods attempt to convert me?"

"No," I said. "I promise."

He opened his door, hugged me, and said maybe it would be best if he stayed home to sort things out with Mom. We looked at each other and both knew that was impossible. But did this stop me from leaving? No, it did not.

After the trout cooks all the way through, I set the cast-iron pan in the dirt and get on my knees. "Dear heavenly Father," I say. And no more words come. I had envisioned this as a prayer for sanity, and for wisdom. I had promised myself I would stay in the woods and the wind and the rain until I stumbled onto the path down which God wanted me to lead my family. Yet now, with just me and the clouds and the smells of forest and sausage and trout, I cannot bring myself to say a simple blessing for my meal.

So I sit cross-legged with a plate on my lap and eat as the dog watches every rise and fall of my fork. His whiskers twitch, and he licks drool from his lips. I set down my plate with half the fish still uneaten, but that dog does not budge until I tell him to go for it. When he leaps up, lightning splits the sky. As he eats, thunder rumbles down the valley. The rain begins, and the girl and her father scramble into their tent. They zip and unzip it and gather their things.

Eventually, at dusk, the sky clears and the girl climbs out onto the highest boulder. She looks down and waves at me and the dog. I want to reach up and wrap a sweater around her shoulders. I pretend not to see her and scoop mud onto the embers of my fire.

Long after the moon goes down, I wake to the girl's father's shouts. He growls and curses at the night. The dog barks, but I put a hand on his head to hush him. I unzip the window flap of my tent. The father's flashlight spins on the hilltop like an airway beacon.

"Watch out," he shouts. "There's a bear out there. Or maybe not a bear, but something big."

I hear nothing but the man's voice and the trickle of the stream. After a while he gives up on me. He and his daughter whisper for a long time, and the dome of their yellow tent glows like a second moon until the sky turns purple and fades into baby blue.

Around noon, the girl arrives at my camp with hugs and kisses for the dog. She tosses pinecones into the stream, and the dog fetches them. Her father shows up, too, with a handful of stone arrowheads. He lets me hold one. It is small and dull and surprisingly heavy. We're not the first ones here, he tells me, and he wipes his neck with a red bandana. What he wouldn't give, he says, to build a house on that ridge.

I ask where he comes from, what he does, and if he knows how lucky he is to have such a bright little girl. He is a contractor without contracts, he says. He comes from Butte, and his daughter isn't half as innocent as she might seem. But it feels right to bring her into the wild, away from friends and computers and a mother who coddles her.

I tell him to never stop coddling her. And, without a thought for how the question might sound, I ask if his daughter likes boys.

Maybe he sees the stress in my eyes or the tightness in my lips. Perhaps he thinks I am a molester or a rapist. Or possibly he just pities me as I fumble his arrowhead to the dirt. But he doesn't pick it up. He tells me to keep it. I, too, leave the arrowhead on the ground. I am in no mood to bend over. The man calls to his daughter, says goodbye, and tells me to watch out for bears.

I hike a mile to the lake. No one is there. A loon touches down on the water. He folds his wings, looks around, and calls over and over for something or someone who never arrives. I toss in a line. The dog sits up and pants. I think about Peter and the mystery of what he has become. I realize that he isn't done becoming. After all, he has three years left of high school, then college, then his whole life. And, really, what has my wife become? Erin has always been deeply religious. Until now I have compensated for her mean streak, pretended it wasn't there. Yet in many ways, she is my rock. I want to be that solid ground for her now, for both of them, but I have no idea how.

I reel in a good-sized rainbow trout, bash its head on a rock, poke a knife into its gills to bleed it, and hike back to camp.

When I get there, the yellow tent is gone from the hilltop. I climb up to see their campsite and find no trace that they were ever there. Then I gut, clean, and fry my trout without the smell of garlic and sausage blowing down the hillside. And the smell is all wrong. So I pack up, hike back to the car, and drive home in the dark.

Passing through Butte, I see Our Lady of the Rockies—a 100-foot-tall Madonna on a cliff above the town. She stands there, all lit up and bursting with love, stretching her concrete arms wide to embrace the world. Surely her gesture is meant to inspire, but it strikes me as weak. It reminds me of me. And for a while I give into the temptation to blame myself for all that has gone wrong. I love Peter and Erin, but emotion alone is not enough. Like the statue, I open my arms, stand tall, and wait for something to happen.

When I get home, the house is silent. I see Peter's light under his door, but I don't hear him moving around in there. So I crawl into bed beside Erin. All night, I dream of bonfires, forest fires, and ashes in rings of stone.

....

Erin and I wake at the same time, eye to eye across the gap between our pillows. She sits up and covers her breasts with the sheet. She asks why I came home so soon then tells me she wants a divorce.

"Can we eat breakfast first?" I ask.

Outside, brakes squeal, a garbage truck's compactor roars to life, and a trash can slams to the street. I pull Erin close. She pulls away, gets out of bed, and wraps the sheet around her body.

"He'll outgrow this," I say. "Give him time."

"No," she says. "I've prayed on it."

"Then give *us* time," I say.

And she says she has prayed on that, too. This is her final word on the subject. She carries her work clothes into the bathroom and locks the door. I push my face into the pillow and feel the dog's wet tongue on the foot I've dangled off the end of the bed.

And for several days—when I'm not boxing up Peter's and my possessions, applying for jobs, or arguing with Erin, whose heart has grown crooked and gnarled with knots—I sample sausages from butcher shops around town. I cook these with trout and sage. Sometimes Erin rallies enough to thank me for these dinners.

Peter, the vegetarian, refuses to try them. They are good meals, but they do not give off the scent I crave. I soon quit red meat in favor of chicken and seafood. And, once the divorce paperwork arrives in the mail, I eat no meat at all because I can no longer shake the image of that trout's eyes as I bashed its head on a rock.

At some point Erin and I find ourselves standing together in the laundry room. She asks why Peter and I still live in her house. I tell her I will not leave until I have everything I need. She asks what that means, and I shrug. She piles dry clothes into a wicker basket. I tell her to stop. Then I get down on one knee and ask her to marry me all over again.

"Come on," I say. "This time at least we'll know what the hell we're getting into."

She puts a hand over her mouth. Then she shuts the dryer, grabs the cordless phone, and locks herself in the bathroom.

....

Four months pass, and I live with my things in the basement. I eat little and cook almost nothing. I've lost forty pounds. When I walk the dog, the neighbors say I am wasting away.

I know now what was missing in my failed attempts to conjure up that elusive odor of sausage, sage, and trout. One simply cannot extract pollen, sap, and mist from the forest air and bring it home. But on winter afternoons, wrapped in the heat of the house, I sometimes stroke the dog and catch myself longing for the smell of that meal. I think about the girl and her father, as if our chance encounter marked a crossroads—as if the odors in the air that night carried meanings I had failed to grasp. I sift through every detail. I shift the angle of a rock and the slant of an arm. I adjust the balance and heft of the gear in my pack. I shuffle the order of moments and string the daughter's words through the mouth of the father—and his words through her mouth—hoping to catch them out in a lie, a dodge, a moment of truth. I fumble around for some toehold on which to scramble back through time and ask that girl and her father in the full light of day to please take my son's faithful, dopey dog as a gift.

Yet I love this dog. I bought him as a pup, a present for Peter's birthday. But Peter ignored him from the start. Now the dog goes wherever I go. He naps with me on the couch in the family room. He rolls in the snow when I shovel the walk. He nuzzles my wife when I pass her in the hall, and he licks Peter's wet shoes after school. And, after the dog has loved them, he sits at my feet and sleeps. I understand now that he is mine, and he shows me the way.

Mallard

Mo might not have been all the way awake when she told me to cut the coughing or she'd kick me out of the damn bed, but it irked me, so I went downstairs, stepped out the back door, climbed the fence, crossed the neighbors' yard, and hoofed it up 29th Street to the drugstore. Which was closed. So I kept going north past the air base converted to a medical campus for toxicity testing of beauty products on the skin of paid volunteers. At the corner of 29th and Pine, I met a duck.

He was a mallard. He looked dazed, standing in a cone of light under a street lamp, like a foreigner in need of directions but without the words to ask. He had a crooked lower beak.

"Hey there," I said. "You all right?"

He stepped toward me, and his shadow grew. I knelt and he waddled over to my knee. His crooked beak wasn't broken or bloodied, just askew. He let me pick him up. His breath puffed into little clouds. I wrapped my sweater around him, with his head through the neck hole, and carried him to the pond at 6th and Gage. He rode along under my arm. His head bobbed with each step I took. I set him down and unwrapped him, and he tottered onto the grass.

"Go on," I said. "Go find your family. Or your tribe. Or your flock. Or whatever."

He looked at the pond then at me.

I put on my sweater and walked away, past the cemetery. The drugstore at the far end of 29th stayed open twenty-four hours. A clerk with glitter in her hair directed me to a shelf of nighttime cough suppressants. I bought the one on sale and walked home.

Lights shone through the windows, upstairs and down. I walked in through the front door. Mo apologized to someone on the phone for the inconvenience and hung up. She asked where the hell I'd gone.

I told her I'd gone out and met a nice duck. Her lip curled. She cinched her bathrobe and took my plastic sack to the counter.

"Aw," she said, when I described the duck's crooked beak. She wrapped me in a fleece blanket and spooned cough syrup into my mouth. I liked the grape flavor. And I liked the way she tipped the spoon and pulled it from my lips, as if it weren't so much the dose that would relieve my lungs but the love.

"You smell like duck," she said.

"Quack," I said.

She tucked me into the sofa and shut off the lights. I could see her standing by the stairs, watching me. After a while, she went up to bed. Shapes in the dark transformed from shadows to lamps, picture frames, a chair, and a grandfather clock. I hatched a plan to fly to Tucson in January, provided I not die of pneumonia first.

In the morning, I drove past the pond. The duck was still there, shuffling from foot to foot on the grassy bank, watching the street, surrounded by geese.

Lavender

As a child, I thought of my mother and father in terms of centuries. This man and this woman had lived forever, it seemed, born wholly formed and unchanging, waiting patiently for me and my sisters to come along. Had someone told me my parents weren't, in truth, much older than I, that they were scarcely more than children themselves, I would have considered it a lie to rival the tooth fairy. Had the liar then taken me to the attic, opened the trunk that held my father's dusty telescope and my mother's moth-eaten Burano lace baby dress, and told me these antiques were almost new, fresh out of the box, I would have laughed. But a span of decades has passed as quickly as smoke from a blown-out candle.

My mother came to visit shortly after my father passed away. On her last night in town, I sat her down and poured shots of tequila. It was past midnight. My wife and daughters had gone to bed. Moths flitted at the window screens. I took the easy chair, and my mother reclined on the sofa with her feet on the coffee table. She watched me drink a second shot, then tipped back her glass and swallowed. As she did this, her blue bathrobe came open a bit at the neck, exposing the freckled V of a tan line and the white frill of her nightgown. She shook her head and set her glass on the corner of a magazine. When she pulled away her fingers, the glass tipped and rolled off the table onto the carpet.

"Oops," she said.

I angled the bottle toward her. "Another?"

She gave a quiet, throaty laugh and waved me away.

I started to pour one for myself but changed my mind and set the bottle on the floor. "So, Mom," I said, "how does it feel to live alone?"

"It's all right," she said and adjusted her lapels. "A good-looking man knocked on my door last week."

I struggled for a proper response and came up with "Oh?"

"He was quite young. Much younger than you. He was selling magazine subscriptions to raise money for something or other." She shut her eyes and tilted her head toward the ceiling as if she heard the call of some faraway bird. "When I was fifteen, a salesman came to the house. He was handsome. Very handsome. This was a Saturday afternoon, and my parents had gone to Columbus to buy a car. I stayed home to study. And this man in a blue suit—very sharp—came in and opened up a suitcase full of flowery soaps."

"I once bought chocolate bars from three different kids in a single afternoon," I said.

"I let him smooth-talk his way into the kitchen," she said. "I shouldn't have, but I did. He seemed harmless enough. And so attractive, the kind of man you'd almost call pretty." She chuckled, rubbed her elbow. "He asked how many boyfriends I had. Inside of ten minutes, he was kissing me right there in my mother's kitchen. Oh, and he smelled of lavender."

She leaned forward, picked up her shot glass, and raised it in the air. I poured us each another shot. Moths tapped at the window screen.

"When I asked where he came from," she said, "he told me the train. That was it, just the train. And he had the softest little mustache."

"I suppose those kids were selling candy bars to raise money for a school band," I said.

"After a few kisses—and this is strictly between you and me—he slipped his hand in my blouse, over the top of my brassiere. And I let him. He had a gold wedding band on his finger, and I could feel it through the bra. It was cold."

"Let's just pause the story right there, Mom."

She breathed, breathed again. "Sorry."

"It's OK."

"No, I shouldn't," she said. "The girls are in bed, right? Good."

Her face flushed for a moment. Her soul fell back from her eyes and her mouth went still. She looked at the floor.

"Shoot," she said after a few seconds. "It's late."

She slid her reading glasses into her pocket and held out her hands for a lift from the sofa. Then she kissed my cheek and walked down the hall to the guest bedroom.

The next day, after the girls and I took her to the airport, I found a bra on the towel rack in the guest bathroom. The bra was white, a matronly style with lots of stitching and padding. Later, I tried to explain to my wife, Carol, why I kept the bra on my closet shelf rather than sending it home to my mother. Carol said I was sweet and a little funny, but holding onto the bra made no sense to her. Eventually we agreed to store it in an old shoe box. It would be our little secret.

Days passed, and months, and our little secret became just another piece of clutter. It stayed on that shelf for three years, until the night we came home from my mother's funeral. I sat in my overstuffed chair with a bottle of whiskey and thought about my daughters. They would start kissing boys in the next couple of years, if they hadn't already. I drank a shot, then another, and went upstairs. With the curtains drawn, the bedroom was pitch-black. I felt my way to the closet, found the shoe box, and opened it. The bra's tiny hooks clicked against the cardboard as I lifted the straps. I pressed my nose to one of the cups, which smelled faintly of potpourri and talcum powder and cardboard. And somehow, in all that lace and stitching, I could smell traces of my mother's skin, her breath, and a cold wedding ring on a soap-scented hand.

Carol sat up in bed. I kissed her and told her to go back to sleep. Then I placed the bra in the shoe box, took the box downstairs to a trunk in the basement, and went to the window to watch the moon sink behind the mountain.

House of Ghosts

The blue Victorian at 1145 White Street shifts in its foundation, creaks, and settles in for the night. The boys are bundled into their beds. My wife, too, has gone to sleep. I'm alone in the kitchen, steeping chamomile tea, coughing phlegm into the lines of my palms. Toast crumbs on the table shiver when I exhale. The refrigerator groans. The candle pops. The back door swings open, and the ghost of my father's lover stands there in the moonlight.

I offer him tea. He accepts and smiles as if death were an exquisite pleasure. I pour hot water into a World's Best Mom mug and tell him it's been five days since the night my wife called me David. I was kissing her breast, and I saw her lips as she whispered it: Oh, David. Her eyes bloomed with the horror of her mistake. Her cheeks turned pink then a pale green.

David, I asked. Who is David?

My father's lover's ghost takes his tea with honey and sips with his pinkie extended. I ask if my father was passionate in bed.

The ghost's gaze trails toward the knife block and the spice rack. He sets down his tea and beckons me to follow. We walk to the back porch. The boards squeak beneath my feet but not his.

Outside, in the yard, everything is gray—the moon, the stars, the decrepit fence. And other silver ghosts are there. My grandfather, in a powder-blue polyester coverall suit, plucks cherries from a branch of my wife's apple tree. My childhood dog Farrell—half mutt, half beagle—naps at my feet. My high school football coach, Butch Stuemke, stands with his arms wrapped around the keg of his chest, watching me, waiting for me to throw a block or catch a pass, to do something, anything.

My father's lover's ghost puts a hand on my shoulder and presses me to take a seat on the steps. He sits behind me, cradles me, and whispers that I am brave to go on living. I rest my head in his lap, and for the first time in five nights I drift toward sleep.

Did he ever talk about me? I ask.

Oh, all the time, the ghost says. He never stopped. You were the most lovable kid in the world. You were his cupid, his darling boy, his perfect little cherub.

I shut my eyes. Something moves in the grass. The ghost strokes my hair. I keep wondering if it will rain.